BROKEN
wings

www.chellebliss.com

CHELLE BLISS

USA TODAY BESTSELLING AUTHOR

BROKEN WINGS © 2022

Publisher © Chelle Bliss September 6th 2022
Edited by Lisa A. Hollett
Proofread by Read By Rose
Cover Design © Chelle Bliss
Cover Photo © Michelle Lancaster @lanefotograf

www.chellebliss.com

CHELLE BLISS

USA TODAY BESTSELLING AUTHOR

CROW

"LOGAN TAYLOR?" THE UNIFORMED OFFICER FISTS A wrinkled paper bag covered in unreadable scribbles. He peers at me through thick glasses, as if the frown lines on my face will somehow match the crap written in black Sharpie.

By now, I'm so used to being called every possible insult, I almost don't respond to my given name. But after spending the last three hours in processing, going through identity verification, and signing on the dotted line over and over again, those two words—Logan Taylor—are starting to feel real again.

Still, hearing my name on Officer Wurst's tobacco-stained lips makes my mouth go sour. At any moment, this bastard could take a swing at me, accuse me of something, and in the blink of an eye, my ass would be back in orange, sharing a stainless-steel toilet with my most recent cellmate, "Nightmare" Nate.

The last seven years of my life in Level 2 lockup have been a living hell, but my cellmate earned the nickname through acts viler than anything I could ever dream of. And yet, there I was, right in the bunk next to him.

But today's the day I pay my debt shit off in full.

"You Taylor?" the officer repeats when I don't respond, looking at me like maybe the endless forms got it wrong.

I almost laugh at the irony. For years, I haven't been myself. Forget about who I once was. That's a very distant memory. But that's not what he's getting at. He's doing his five-figure-a-year job plus bennies making sure the right asshole is released today.

Nothing more, nothing less.

So I choke back the bile and nod. "That's me, sir." Tacking "sir" on to the end like it means something. I just hope I don't sound like I'm sucking up to him—or worse, being sarcastic.

Wurst has never done anything to earn my respect, but I'll kiss his ass and call him Mama if that means putting this place behind me even a minute faster. I can tolerate the game to reach what's on the other side of that locked door.

Freedom.

Wide blue sky, endless groves of orange trees, and miles of green grass, unmarred by barbed wire and armed guards. It's all so close, I can practically taste the sweet Florida citrus on my tongue.

I try not to look at Wurst's oily hairline and wait for whatever it is that comes next so I can walk through that security door.

"Got all your personal effects? Unless you want to go back?" He cackles at his own joke.

I look him over skeptically. As if there is anything from that sickly green concrete room that I'd want to take out of here.

The truth is… There's nothing.

While this place held me in a choke hold, I let parts of me die to survive.

My pride.

My dignity.

My sense of myself as a man.

Like a helpless baby, I ate the slop they spooned into my mouth. Swallowed nonstop bullshit they rained down on not just me, but all of us. How weak, useless, and ruined we all were. How we're the lowest of the low, no good to anyone. Never was, never would be.

I took the abuse and the violence, the loneliness and the monotony, because taking it meant I'd make it to this moment.

And I sure as hell am not about to say or do

anything to fuck that up now. The only thing between me and that endless blue outside is one more guard. One more hoop. One more question.

I nod and give him the answer I know he wants.

"Donated my books back to the library," I say. "I'm good to go."

I hold up my hands to show there's nothing I'm hiding. Nothing in the pockets of the stiff thrift store jeans and scratchy, ill-fitting T-shirt provided for me by the state on my release.

"All righty, then." Wurst waddles past me. "Follow me."

I keep my distance walking behind him. It's surreal not being restrained by some kind of shackles as I head down a narrow corridor. I shuffle along, keeping my eyes low and my expectations lower. If my dad and brother could see me now… I thanked God every day I was locked up that no one from my family came to see me. Not once.

A couple of calls from my dad and brother my first few weeks in. One deposit into my commissary account. That's it. That's all the support my family gave me over the years. They left me to rot in hell, believing I got what I deserved for what went down.

And that's how I preferred it.

Nothing about me being here was *justice*. My sentence—downgraded from the minimum set by

Florida law due to the circumstances—was about making somebody pay, plain and simple. If consequences were fair, if there were any such thing as real justice, well, a lot of things would have been very, very different.

I'm not saying I didn't do the crime. I sure as fuck did. I swung a punch in a bar and shattered the face of a man who more than deserved it. He literally asked for it.

But the state of Florida had a dead man on their hands and witnesses who ID'd me as the one who threw the fatal punch. Not the first punch, mind you. But the last. Witnesses backed up my version of the story, but truth doesn't matter when there's a bar fight, a dead man, and a guy left standing with blood on his hands.

Facts… Fuck the facts.

Two men died that shitty summer night. The minute I threw that punch, my life was over. Not the same kind of over as that meth head from the bar, but over just the same.

I was arrested, tried, and convicted. *Lucky* to get seven years, reduced from the state minimum for manslaughter because of a carve-out in the law. I accepted the judge's "mercy," the two and a quarter years he shaved off my sentence because the victim contributed to the circumstances that led to his own harm.

The state took away my work, my freedom, years of

my life on this earth because I stopped a guy hopped up on drugs from terrorizing a couple of idiot kids who were in the wrong place at the wrong time. I could have walked away or ordered another beer and tucked into a dark corner like so many of the witnesses there that night. But if there's one thing my father raised me to do —aside from knowing when to call a man sir—it was to jump in and help when needed.

"Be an example, son," he'd say. "When others run away, real men run in."

I ran in, all right. Fists flying.

And every day since, I've had a lot of time to think about what a *real man* is. What a hero is. And whether that's what I want to be.

I could have gotten my life back several times over, but I made no effort to get released early. Refused parole, wanted nothing to do with probation. No ties to bind me to this hell. When I walk out of here, I want to be truly free. Accountable to no one but myself and to the brotherhood. The fact that there is any brotherhood left waiting for me is a shock.

My cheap sneakers—another parting gift from the Florida Department of Corrections—squeak on the tile floor on that long, quiet walk to the exit.

I start panicking.

This is real. I'm getting the fuck out.

I take a long last breath of stale, institutional air and

blink hard. Not once, not twice, but again and again to make sure the door unlocking in Wurst's hand is really happening. Not a dream I'll wake up from. This is it. I can believe what I'm seeing because it's finally happening.

Wurst calls into a radio at his shoulder and nods. "All right, man." He holds out a paper bag, and I just stare at it, eyes locked on his hand.

I'm ashamed to admit it, but I'm afraid to take it from him. My instincts after all this time so trained to submit, to seem harmless, to disappear in a sea of far more dangerous faces, that I can't even grab what rightfully belongs to me.

The guard makes it easy on me, shoving the wrinkled mess into my hands.

"Your commissary account's been cashed out." He points at the bag. "There's a prepaid card in there with your balance on it."

I'm tempted to open the bag to make sure, but I'm not going to risk pissing the guy off.

"Hope to never see you again, Taylor," he says, and there's a bit of kindness in words. Like, maybe, he really means it.

I nod to him. "Yes, sir," I say, because saying anything else is only going to tempt everything inside me to come pouring out. And right now, I need to keep my cool. I'm still on government property.

Wurst holds the door open and squawks into his radio so the guards monitoring the perimeter know I've got the okay to leave.

"Johnson!" Wurst shouts to the van driver. He's smoking a cigarette and looking pissed off that his break has been interrupted. "Just one today."

"Ahh right, ahh right." The guy stubs out his cigarette and gets behind the wheel. "Let's do this, then. Gives me an excuse to get out of this sun."

I look between Wurst and Johnson, in disbelief that they aren't going to lock me into the van. Monitor my every move until I'm secure in my seat where I can't be a threat to anyone. Why would they? I'm technically a free citizen now. All that's left to do is transport me off the property. But it still feels fucking crazy.

I scan the road ahead, the service drive that leads a long loop around the facility, where family members and friends park for visiting days and for times just like this. I debate just walking to the visitor lot. No one will be waiting for me there, not yet. There's no rush to get where I'm going.

But then I think about the thousand things that could happen between here and there and decide following the protocol is the easiest way to make sure my last day in prison stays my last day. I shove aside my fears that this transport is a trick my mind is playing on me, or worse, a trick the guards are playing on me.

I'm getting out. It's all but done.

I climb in the rear, slam the door shut behind myself, and sit my ass in a seat. I wonder if the view will look any different as a free man. The only times I've been in this vehicle I've been heavily monitored and shackled. And then I realize I haven't buckled my seat belt. I do it quick, even though it's a very short ride. Johnson's still a cop after all.

Once he starts up the van, I get nauseous. A combination of so, so many things. But Johnson's a chatterer, so I focus on him and not the waves of worry sloshing in my gut.

"Congrats, man." Johnson's so relaxed, making small talk, his arm slung out the window. "You got a woman waiting for you?"

I swallow hard and wonder if I'm really going to be sick. "Don't know," I say. A vague response is better. Nothing could be further from the truth. I've got no one waiting for me. And the last thing on my mind is getting a piece of ass. I'm still too focused on getting out of here with my ass intact in this set of cheap pants instead of an orange jumpsuit, but agreeing with him is the path of least resistance.

Within minutes, we're pulling into a parking lot. Johnson leans out to chitchat with the guard on duty at the lot. I'm not sure if I'm free to get out, so I sit there, seat belt on, awaiting instructions.

"Hey!" Johnson calls out, giving me a wave. "You're all good, man." He points toward the street, an empty two-lane highway. "Bus will be by at some point."

Johnson goes back to chatting up the other guard, so I open the back door and step out. Just like that. Hand on the handle. My foot on the pavement.

I turn slowly and shut the door behind me, every muscle in my body burning with tension. I grip the paper bag in my hand, my knuckles white. The same knuckles that got me sent here in the first place.

I relax my hands. Roll my shoulders. Take in a lungful of fresh air.

Then I turn my back on the prison, the van, Johnson…all of it. And I walk away.

"You fuckin' bastard." A black extended cab pickup truck slows to a stop about ten feet away from me. The window's rolled down, and a heavily tattooed arm flips me off.

When the driver's side door opens, a man about my size climbs out, his motorcycle boots pounding hard on the hot concrete. His muscular arms are exposed, but I cock my head when I realize he's not wearing his leathers. No vest. No patch.

"You fuckin' pussy," I reply. "What the hell happened to you?"

Morris, the VP of the Disciples, crosses his arms over the chest of a short-sleeved black golf shirt. He looks down at himself and scrubs a hand over his chin.

"Lot has changed, man," he says, a grin twisting his lips.

The passenger door opens, and a man who has no business fitting his massive girth into a pickup truck stumbles out.

"Tiny." I nod. "Good to see some things haven't changed."

Tiny pulls a toothpick from between his teeth and snorts. "Just you wait, brother. Just you fucking wait."

Morris comes at me in a run. He tackles me at full speed and sticks a shoulder in my chest before wrapping his arms around me in a hug. "Been waiting long, you son of a bitch?"

I stiffen at the shouting, at the contact, but try to slow my breathing to remind myself this is cool. I can be cool. To these guys, nothing's changed. It's just been a minute since we've seen one another. Still Disciples. Still brothers.

I pound Morris on the back and notice as he pulls away that there's a wedding ring on his hand. "What in the name of…?"

"Told you." Tiny lumbers over to clap me in the world's sweatiest hug. "Talk about a ball and chain."

"You asshole," Morris says, shaking his head. "Way too soon for prison jokes." He smacks Tiny playfully across the back. "This one should talk. Come on, we've got a lot to catch you up on." Morris looks at the paper sack in my hands. "That your shit?"

I nod, suddenly regretting letting Morris and Tiny pick me up. Once I was scheduled for release, they insisted, but I'd been so focused on getting out of prison, I hadn't even thought about how I'd feel physically going home. Seeing people I knew again. I didn't know if I knew myself anymore, let alone these two. But it's only been five minutes since they rolled into the lot, and Morris is grabbing me by the shoulders and shaking me. Hard.

"It's fucking good to have you back, brother." Something like tears glimmers in his eyes. "We've missed you, Crow."

Hearing my old name brings water to my eyes, but there is no way I am going to let it flow. I let Morris hug me again, and then Tiny plants a meaty palm against my back.

"Come on, brother," he says. "Let's get your ass home."

I climb into the back of Morris's truck and roll down the window first thing. After being locked down for so many years, the last thing I want is to be closed up in a small space for a long ride, even a truck with two of my oldest friends.

Morris and Tiny yammer up front, talking about things and people I have never heard of and know nothing about. They include me, calling back to me, asking me about everyday things like food and getting me a phone.

It's overwhelming. I shut down and just nod, listening to what they say while the fresh air messes up my hair on the drive back to the compound.

I'm sure I'll adjust. I'll adapt. Just like I did inside. But right now, despite the fluffy clouds overhead and the brilliant sun on my face, I'm like a bird whose wings have been clipped. After dreaming of the flight for so, so long, I feel like I'm falling. That feeling doesn't ease when we pull into the parking lot of the compound.

The three of us head inside on a much different vibe than the one I left on. I remember that day too clearly, but I refuse to think about that now.

When Morris yanks open the door and shoves me inside, it's this surreal feeling, almost like time travel. The place is familiar and so much the same, but it's been so, so long, it's hard to believe it's real. And then I hear the screams.

The first person I see when I walk in is Madge. Her stream of curse words would put my cellmate's colorful vocabulary to shame. But by the time I'm all the way through the door, she's got her arms around me and is holding me tight.

"Oh my freaking God. You're a goddamn sight for sore eyes, Crow," she says.

She sounds genuinely happy to see me, even though it's been a lifetime. People finish college in the time I've been gone. Shit, med students become doctors. Kids finish almost an entire primary education. The world is a very different place than it was when I left it. I can see and hear it already. But if Madge is any indication, some things didn't change much at all.

"Hey," I say, tentatively at first. I'm not sure where my words are. Where my old vibe went. I used to talk a certain way to women, back when women were plentiful in my life and not carrying weapons to take my ass down if I so much as looked at them sideways.

She's holding me tight and rocking back and forth, but my hands are in the air. I pat her on the back until she finally releases me and looks into my face with what I think are tears in her eyes.

"What happened to you... That whole godforsaken mess... It's over now, Crow. And I'm going to make you a casserole to celebrate." Her words are so unexpected. Kind. Warm. Sincere. Things I've had very little of and don't really know how to respond to.

She turns and bustles away, but Morris clamps a hand on my shoulder and tugs me close.

"Listen, sexy," he says to her, pouring on the charm. "I know it's been a while since Crow enjoyed a Madge special, but our brother's got dinner plans." He nods at me. "Rain check that casserole."

He steers me away from Madge while Tiny walks past and calls out to anyone who's around, "Hey, assholes. Crow's home."

"Mammoth here?" I ask, looking around.

Tiny shakes his head.

"He left when he and Tamara got serious. She's not around either, so you can stop looking around like your head's on a swivel."

"I wasn't looking for her."

Tiny crosses his arms, raising an eyebrow. "You told her you were going out of state to do your time in order to lure her to the prison. Don't look me in the eye and say you weren't making a play for her even back then."

I shrug. "A man's got to try, brother."

"She's off-limits. She's happy and so is Mammoth."

He doesn't need to say anything else. That ship sailed the day she showed up at the compound and I decided to be a dick to her. I drove her right into Mammoth's arms, and he deserved her more than I did. They were right for each other.

Within seconds, Dog and Eagle are thundering

through the compound, lifting me up, arms around my chest. The hugs and the shouts and the enthusiasm surround me, and for a moment, it almost feels normal. I can remember the last time I was here, surrounded by my brothers. That was a hell of a different day. A somber farewell. The end of my life as I knew it.

This should bring shit full circle. And yeah, the feeling of being welcomed back is good, but I know not to get too attached to it. Anything good in my life, I have to be really, really careful with.

I know how easily it can all just disappear.

2

BRIDGET

ONE MONTH LATER…

When I wake up, I don't even have to open my eyes to know it's there. The aura.

Shit. Not today. Please, not today.

The shimmer of color seeping around the edges of my consciousness. Like the prelude to a dream, I see a soft halo behind my eyes as I groan and clench the sheets in my hands.

I try to relax my body and unclench my hands. Breathe deeply through my nose, into my chest, and try to release the tension I'm holding in my face. I know none of this will have any impact on what's coming.

Migraines can't be coaxed, begged, or bullied away, but sometimes I can slow them down with deep breathing and paying attention to where I'm holding in stress.

Today is a day I cannot let this slow me down. I have to get in front of the headache. This is literally my last chance, and if I screw up, I will be out of a job. Unemployed. And in even deeper financial shit than I am already.

The morning sun is just starting to peek past the shades, so I tug the blanket over my eyes and try to tell myself I've got this. I'm prepared for the meeting. I'm going to be okay. I just have to take this morning one minute at a time and not let my emotions, my stress, and my pain take over.

If only I were that powerful.

I fold my hands over my chest and check in with my body. I'm all right. It's just an aura. A little push behind my eyes reminding me to take it easy.

I get out of bed slowly…very slowly. I shove aside the blankets and open my eyes, focusing on the ceiling and nothing else. Then I wiggle my toes and fingers, letting my body wake up and get the blood moving. Ever so gently, I sit up and get out of bed.

It's early, earlier than the alarm would get me up, but since I'm awake now, I silence my device so Mia can have a little extra sleep. Times like this, I wonder what it would be like to have a partner. Forget about the love and, hell, even the sex. Having someone to share these things with. The morning routine. The fear and the uncertainty.

Sigh.

Feels like a dream for other women. Not me.

My last hot relationship, now that I think about it, was with Mia's dad. Bryan was a man I had the good sense never to marry. I only wish I'd had a little less tequila and a lot more self-control during those few weeks I let him into my bed.

Bryan was everything I wanted eight years ago—gorgeous, the life of the party, and horny as all hell. Back then, I was newly legal and hit the bars like any college senior would. I had a great internship, an ID that would finally get me into any bar in the state of Florida, and my whole future ahead of me.

When Bryan ground up against me on the dance floor, his sandy blond hair over his eyes, my fate was sealed.

Thankfully, after all the shit Mom had been through with my dad—none of it her fault—I'd never moved out. Even after Mia arrived, my mom let us live with her. And the three of us did okay for a long time. But things change.

Everything flows and nothing stays.

That was my momma's favorite saying. She started saying it as a way to forgive my dad when he finally admitted he had a whole second family a couple counties over. It was the most messed-up situation, the way my mom found out.

That saying sure was true with Bryan. He was unemployed when I met him, and when he did work, cleaning pools didn't bring in enough to help with child-care and groceries. He flows in and out of my life, having a "boisterous uncle" type of relationship with Mia, but he never stays. He can't be relied on to pay child support, to pick her up from school. I have sole legal custody, but that's never stopped him from drop-ping in on us if he's driving by and stealing Mia away for ice cream.

Everything flows and nothing stays.

Not Bryan and, sadly, not my momma either.

When my mom was around, I didn't worry as much about money, about childcare, or about whether or not Bryan had been around to see his daughter in months, weeks, or days.

But since Mom's been gone, everything has seemed darker, harder. And today's a day that I could use her strength. Her faith in everything turning out okay.

I walk softly down the hallway to the bathroom, moving gently because any sudden move can change this "might be a headache" to a full-on attack by my body on my brain.

I flip on the bathroom light and squint against the intensity of the halo that lights up behind my eyelids.

"I've got this," I tell myself and shove aside the shower curtain.

I turn on the water and decide on a shower. A bath feels like less effort, but I'm worried if I get down into the tub, it'll be too hard for me to get up alone. I let the water splash across my belly, breasts, and gently wash my face.

Once I start to lather my hair, it's clear that nothing I do is going to slow this train. This migraine's got me in its cross hairs, and I now need to outrun it.

My hand is shaking, or maybe it just feels that way, as I turn off the water and grab a towel. I blot my face and leave my hair dripping, just a towel over my shoulders to soak up the water flowing from my long hair. Bending and wrapping my head is literally the last thing I can do. I'll put my hair in a very loose wet bun if that's what it takes to get out of the house today.

"Mia…" I sigh and check the time.

Still wrapped in my towels, I shove open her bedroom door. A mermaid nightlight glows a soft blue on her bedside table. My daughter's bare foot sticks out from beneath the covers, and her blankets are tangled like she went ten rounds in her sleep, trying to fight her way through her dreams.

"Baby," I whisper to keep the volume of my voice quiet as it bounces inside my head. "Time to get up for school."

I stroke her leg and shove aside the mess of blankets. She lifts her eyebrows as though she's having a tough time opening her eyes.

"Okay, Mama," she breathes.

"Are your clothes all ready?" I ask.

She nods into her pillow and then opens her eyes fully. "I picked out the glittery donut dress last night. Can I wear tights?"

I smile. My big girl loves wearing dresses with tights, even running around in the Florida heat. But she's seven, so I let her suffer for fashion as long as the consequences aren't too severe. "Of course."

It kills me, but I don't bend down to kiss her face, worried that anything I do to send blood to my head will speed up the arrival of the headache that's looming. "I'm going to get dressed and make breakfast."

I walk into my room and pull on a pencil skirt and a plain white blouse. My wet hair is going to drip all over the work blouse, so I grab a dry towel from the hall closet and wrap it over my shoulders like a shawl.

I head downstairs, slowly gripping the handrail like I'm ninety and not twenty-nine. At the bottom of the stairs, Mia's backpack is ready to go, but I need to get her lunch and snacks from the fridge. I tiptoe through the quiet home, saying a prayer to the headache gods.

"I just have to make it through the day," I say. "Then I can come home and climb into bed."

I desperately want a little coffee, but making it feels

like too much effort. If I leave the house a few minutes early, I can grab coffee at work after I drop off Mia. There's a snack shop in the lobby of my building. Their coffee tastes stale, but it's there as a last resort if I get desperate. And I am desperate. I'm already on a performance plan. A PIP, as my boss so casually likes to call it. As if a happy-sounding little acronym changes what it means.

Performance Improvement Plan.

I take Mia's lunch box and snack from the fridge and set them on top of her backpack, counting the number of sick days I've taken in the last three months alone. My head hurts too much for math, but it's a lot—too many. My work is exceptional when I'm in the office, but between my own headaches and Mia having a tough time adjusting to life without her grandma, it's true. My performance could use a hell of a lot of improvement. Well, maybe not my performance, but my attendance. The real estate company I work for doesn't have enough employees to have a whole HR department, so it's just Jeff, the owner, and his grandfather running roughshod over my attendance record.

"If we had a three-strike rule, you'd have been gone two or three times over, Birdie."

I check my phone and note the time. We need to get moving, but speed is the last thing I have working for me today.

I head back up the stairs and stop by the bathroom, where Mia is trying to pull a brush through a particularly gnarly-looking tangle.

"Oh God, honey. Stop." I grab the detangling spray and saturate the knot, then take a turn with the brush, trying to work through the mess. "What did you do?" I ask, trying not to hurt her scalp as I pick at the knot. "Roll around in bed all night?"

She nods. "I had a lot of weird dreams."

I grab a sparkly hair tie from the vanity drawer and pull her hair into a ballerina-style bun on the top of her head. That tangled mess in the back will require time and patience. The kind of time and patience I don't have. Not with a morning staff meeting and the threat of a headache pounding in my skull.

"What kinds of dreams?" I ask. I'm pretty sure I already know. The same nightmares that have made her miss school and me miss work after many sleepless nights. But I ask anyway.

She shrugs. "You know."

Mia started having nightmares when my migraines came back about six months ago. I tried to hide the fact that I was struggling from her, but after too many hours in the bathroom or in bed, I had to admit the truth. It's been a couple of months of these symptoms, and the migraines are definitely back.

I smooth the loose tendrils of hair into her bun.

"Baby," I say, even though my Mia is a big girl of seven. "Mama gets headaches sometimes. I know they can be pretty scary, but they aren't serious. You don't have to be afraid. You know what to do if I get really sick."

She nods. "Take your phone and call one of my friends' moms."

"Which one would you call first?" I ask.

"Sophia's."

I smile. "And do you know how to find Sophia's mom in my phone?"

She nods.

"And what if no one answers when you call? If it's a real emergency and you're really scared, what do you do?"

"Call 9-1-1."

"Exactly," I say, trying to give her an overly big smile. "But you're not going to have to do that. I feel okay, and I promise I'm going to get myself checked out by a doctor soon. We'll see if we can't do something to stop this altogether." I take her sweet face in my hands, but as I bend down, I feel it. The throbbing feeling that started off shallow, like a pulse in my temple, quickly goes deep.

The room darkens, and the halo around my vision clouds out my daughter's face.

Shit. Not today. Please, please, not today.

I assure myself I'm okay, because if I start to panic, it will hit me ten times as hard and fast as it might otherwise.

My phone starts ringing, and thankfully, I've got it with me. I set down the hairbrush and glare at the caller ID.

"Good morning, Jeff," I say, trying to keep my voice level.

"Bridget, can you come in an hour early this morning? I looked over your projections, and I'm not comfortable with your analysis of the Q1 numbers. I'd like to…"

I tune out my boss as the impossibility of his request hits me. In order to be at the office an hour early, I'd have to have another mother drop Mia off at school and leave for the office now. I've told Jeff this a thousand times over the last few months, but I've been so focused on keeping this job, I haven't had the nerve to say no to anything extra he's asked. Saying I can't come in early is something I shouldn't even have to do, but here I am, squeezing my eyes closed as I head down the stairs.

"Jeff," I say, trying to break in and interrupt him. But he's talking about my data, and he's talking so loud and so fast. My stomach lurches, and I reach for the handrail.

"Bridget, I really think…" My boss's voice echoes in my ears, the sharp edges of his tone breaking through the walls I've put up around my headache. His words beat at my eardrums, and I hold the phone away, trying to put some space between the sounds and the pounding that's leveling up fast in my skull.

I don't even know how it happens, but before I know it, I'm stumbling. My foot catches on that same old stair with the loose carpeting I've been meaning to fix for months now but haven't had the money.

I stumble forward, grabbing the handrail, but I feel the impact of the banister against my eyebrow and forehead. After the shock of the impact passes, I realize I didn't just stumble...I'm hurt.

"Oh my God!" Blood drips down my face where I've cut my eyebrow. My white dress shirt is spotted with stains, and the red color against the clean white fabric sends my stomach into a tailspin. The towel falls from my shoulders onto the carpeted stair beneath my feet, and my wet hair drips onto my shirt, making the blood spread out.

I drop my phone, vaguely aware of it falling over the side of the banister and hitting the tile of the first floor below.

"Mia," I call out weakly. I don't want to scare her, but the fact is, I'm scared.

The room is starting to spin, and even though my stomach is empty, I'm sure I'm going to be sick.

I grip the wall with my left hand and cover my

mouth with my right as I stumble back upstairs. Mia is in her room, struggling with her tights.

"Mommy has to use the bathroom, honey. I'll take you to school as soon as I'm done."

I shut her bedroom door. If at all possible, I don't want her to hear this. I close the bathroom door just in time to make it to the toilet before the heaving starts. I see colors behind my eyes, and all I feel is pain.

If Jeff's still talking on my phone, he might realize by now that I'm not responding. I'm starting to accept that I'm not making it to work today. Mia's not going to make it to school. I start negotiating with myself.

You can do this. You're okay. Don't think about the job. Right now, just think about getting through this.

I have to get better. I just have to.

When the heaving subsides, I wipe my face and rinse my mouth, then knock on Mia's bedroom door.

"I'm ready," she says as she rushes past me, thundering down the stairs. "I just have to put on my shoes."

"Honey." My voice is weak, but with the pain, the colors, and the nausea, I can't muster the strength to shout. "Mia…"

But she's already downstairs, jamming her lunch bag and snacks into her backpack. "Mom," she calls, "can I wear these?"

She holds up a pair of shoes. They're not on her feet

yet, but they have little lights in the heels that flash with every step. I hold up a hand.

"Honey, not those, maybe don't…"

At the top of the stairs, something I don't expect happens. My heart starts racing, and I feel like the room flips over in front of me. Turns out, it's not my eyes playing tricks on me. It's not the pounding in my brain or the twists and turns of my stomach.

"Mama, what happened to your face? Why are you bleeding?" Mia is staring up at me, looking terrified.

I try to reassure her, but the words are like cotton in my mouth. I feel the sensation of falling, and I'm watching my daughter's face as tears wet her cheeks.

"I'm okay, honey." I try to tell her I'm okay, but I'm definitely not okay. "Can you grab my phone?" The words come out thick and heavy, my tongue like a lazy worm, wiggling back and forth in my mouth, but not doing exactly what I want.

I try to sit down on the top step so I don't fall completely down the stairs, but I feel movement all around me, more sharp blasts against my face and skull. I lift my hands to protect myself, but it's as if my body is no longer mine to control. I feel pain and weakness, sickness, and spinning. And then, before I figure out exactly what's happening, everything goes dark.

3

CROW

I wake up to three texts I really don't want to see.

One of the texts is from Arrow, this guy who runs a small PI agency in the strip mall the Club owns. Morris hooked me up with Leo and Tim at the auto body shop, but it's only part time.

Arrow wants me to come work for him. Full-time hours, good pay. Some shitty overpriced health insurance plan, but it'll be better than prison doctors. The thing is, he wants me to work the street with him. Take pics of cheating husbands and people bilking their workers' comp for more payouts long after they're healthy enough to go back to work.

Something about the whole thing feels...too close to criminal activity. Maybe it's not. Maybe I should give that shit a try and just consider all the options, but something like what Arrow's doing somehow doesn't sit right. So I swipe away the notification of the text from him and groan at Leo's message.

Sorry, man. Slow day today. Will text tomorrow if we need an extra set of hands.

So now, I'm out of work for the day, with nothing but time to fill. Fuck if this doesn't feel a lot like prison in that way.

The third text, I delete without reading. It's from my brother, and I'm in no position to connect with my family yet. I may be out, but I'm not ready to talk to my brother or listen to my dad. They let me rot without contact for years. I was glad for it, because other than talking about the latest flavor of instant noodles at the commissary, there was literally nothing to say to my dad. Retired military. Active in local politics back home in New York. We had nothing in common before when I was a grease monkey spending all my free time and money on women and bikes. Now? That I have a record, no job, and not much more than a cell phone to my name?

"Hey there, sexy." Madge is in the kitchen of the compound making coffee. "You're up early again. You know you can sleep in now. Nobody's blowing a whistle or smacking the bars to wake you up."

I know Madge means well, but the prison jokes just

don't land for me. It's not that it's too soon. It's always going to be a sore spot.

I give her a wave and, without a word, slide a pair of sunglasses over my eyes.

When I was locked up, I worked out with weights and sometimes played basketball in the yard. But every time I think about going out back and lifting weights in the compound yard, something inside me panics.

So, I've taken up a new hobby.

The road open before me.

Sun on my face and wind in my hair.

A sense of freedom.

Now, I run.

Sunglasses over my face, I head out into the morning. I sprint past the compound grounds, down the long road, and through the surrounding neighborhood, pounding my feet hard and gripping my hands into fists. I sweat and run until my body burns and the muscles in my thighs tell me I have to stop. I break in the middle of a block, bend over, and rest my hands on my knees, gasping for air.

I take a breath and keep going. I run farther, never faster, every day training myself to go another block. Another two blocks. Past a house with a blue door. Past a yellow car. Anything and everything I can do to push myself ahead, to go farther today than I did yesterday... To find a small, attainable landmark in the distance that I can reach. To me, that's progress. On some level, if I can do it this way, maybe I can do it in other areas of my life too.

Today, I set my sights crazy far. I don't know why. My skin itches and my hair drips sweat into my eyes, but the ache inside me is deeper today, urging me to push myself, maybe until I physically can't go any farther. Until I can't feel the failure weighing down on me.

I see a beat-up red car and decide that will be my next break. I'm going to sprint to the car. Give it all I've got. And then, I'll walk back. Catch my breath. Use the couple of bucks I tucked inside Morris's armband with my phone and grab a bottle of water or a coffee on the way back to the compound. Then it'll be time to shower and face another day. But the next few blocks are my therapy. I won't check my phone, won't delete texts. No one is waiting for me, and no one is expecting anything.

I'm alone and as close to alive as I feel these days.

I take off running, eyes set dead ahead on the red car. As I get close to it, I see a little girl out in the yard, but I mind my business and stay focused on the goal.

Red car. Blot out the pain. Ignore the fresh burn in my chest and thighs as I run away, run toward, fuck, as I just *run*. Nobody to stop me. Nobody to tell me I can't go there or I've gone too far. The fact that I can run where I want to, without the threat of punishment behind me, is a gift I don't think I'll ever stop appreciating.

When I reach the car, I stop, fully winded, but I hear through my breathing that the little kid is in a full-on meltdown.

"Help me! Somebody, please!"

The hair on the back of my neck stands on end, and I debate for a split second not getting involved, but I can't leave her here.

"Hey, where're your parents?" I ask.

"I can't find her phone to call 9-1-1. She's just lying there…" She speaks so fast, I barely understand the words.

"What happened?"

"She fell. Please, help her."

I yank the phone from my armband. "You need a phone?" I ask. "You need to call 9-1-1?"

She nods and doesn't hesitate before walking across the yard and meeting me on the sidewalk.

"Thank you," she says, her voice so weak and small I don't know how she's going to talk if she can make that call.

"Yeah, yeah, sure."

I unlock the device and hand her the phone. I look over my shoulder and can't shake the feeling that this is trouble just waiting to find me.

My stomach flips over and my legs tense like I want

to run away, but the kid's small hand is shaking as I see her carefully type in 9-1-1.

As soon as she punches in those numbers and hits send, everything inside me starts to panic. She's using my phone to call the paramedics. Maybe the cops. They'll have my number and this location. And they'll be coming here.

It's okay, I assure myself. *I haven't done anything wrong. As soon as she hangs up, I'll take the phone and run off. I'll be gone before they get here.*

"Just tell them you borrowed a neighbor's phone," I say, but the little girl is already talking to a dispatcher and doesn't hear a word I said.

"I'm seven," she explains. She glances up at me and looks a little confused but then answers whatever the dispatcher asks with, "Yes. Okay. Hold on." The kid holds the phone out to me. "They want to talk to a grown-up."

I freeze and stare at the phone like it's somehow going to attack me. I can hear the dispatcher calling through the line. "Is anyone there? Honey, can you put a grown-up on?"

"Yeah," I bark into the phone as soon as I take it from the little girl. "We need an ambulance." I hope they'll just send EMS and no squad car.

The operator starts asking me the usual questions.

First, my name. Goddammit, that's the one thing I don't want to give.

"Logan Taylor," I snap.

She wants to know where we are.

"The address?" I repeat.

I look up and down the block, searching for street signs. There are a couple black metal numbers on the front of the house, the one with the door partway open, so I read the numbers off to the operator. Then I repeat it, looking at the little girl, and she nods, confirming that I got the number and street right.

"Okay, sir, now can you describe the injuries? Can you tell me what happened while I dispatch EMS?"

"Hang on," I say. I hit mute on the phone and ask the kid, "What's your name? Your mom's name? They want to know what happened."

"I'm Mia," she says. "My mom's Birdie. Bridget Connor, but everyone calls her Birdie."

"Ma'am?" I unmute the phone. "I've got Mia Connor here..." I look at the kid because I didn't confirm that her last name was the same as her mom's. Could be anything. But she nods, so I go on. "Her mother Bridget took a fall on the stairs."

The dispatcher starts talking over me. "All right, sir, I need you to..." She starts asking me specific questions, like is she bleeding, is she breathing, so I look at little Mia.

"Can you take me to your mom? The 9-1-1 lady is sending help, but I need to see your mom."

Mia nods and breaks into a full run.

I unmute the phone. "On our way to her now."

I jog to the front door and peek inside. When I see a woman lying on a cold tile floor, blood on her shirt and the floor, I don't hesitate.

I motion Mia away. "Honey, why don't you step aside and give your mama some air." I kneel down beside the woman and quickly try to piece together what I see. The woman's dressed professionally in a white shirt and pencil skirt. There's a cut on her forehead right at the eyebrow, and I'm pretty sure that's what's caused all the blood. Her hair is wet, and there's a towel on the steps. I scan the staircase and see the old carpet, and the best I can piece together is that what the kid said is what happened.

"Ma'am?" I say to the dispatcher. "I'm with her."

"All right, sir, is she conscious? Is she breathing?"

"Breathing, yeah. But she's not conscious."

"All right, is she bleeding? Any signs of visible injuries?"

"She's got a cut on her eyebrow, and—" I kneel down beside her on the tile "—yes, she's bleeding."

"All right, I've dispatched an ambulance. They should be there within four minutes, but I'd like you to put some pressure on the wound to help control the bleeding." The dispatcher keeps me on the line, asking me all kinds of questions—how she's sitting, if I can get her to speak.

"Birdie," I say, remembering what the kid said her mom's name was. "Birdie, can you hear me?"

I've got the phone in one hand, and with the other, I take the towel and press it against her wound. She murmurs in response, which I take as a very good sign.

Mia drops to her knees beside her mom and grabs her hand. "Mama, please get up!"

I motion to Mia to step back, and in that moment, my instincts kick in. "The ambulance is going to be here soon, so can you find your mom's purse? And if you know where she keeps her keys, she's going to need them."

Mia nods and rushes off to find those things, while I return my attention to Bridget.

"Bridget, Birdie…" I don't know what to call her, but I try any name she might respond to. "Help is on the way, okay? Can you try to open your eyes?"

She flutters her lids and groans. "Mia," she mumbles. "My daughter…"

"Mia is fine," I assure her.

Mia comes back with her mom's purse and keys. She hands them to me as if I'll know what to do with them.

"Good girl," I say, my voice tight.

The dispatcher is asking questions, but I'm only half listening.

Mia is crying and looks like she's going to lose it, so I scramble my brain to think of another job for her to do. Anything to keep the kid focused on something other than her mom.

"Mia," I say gently. "Do you have a favorite toy or book you want to bring to the hospital? When the paramedics come, they will probably want to take your mom to a doctor, so you'll want to bring along some things to play with. Can you do that?"

Mia nods slowly but then dashes up the stairs and disappears into one of the bedrooms.

"Mia…" Bridget is moaning, but she must be coming to. She lifts a hand to her eyes but then covers her mouth. "I'm going to be sick."

Oh fuck.

I drop the phone and grab her hand. I help her sit up just in time for her to vomit on the tile. Nothing much comes out, just a little saliva, but she groans like she's in agony at the movement. I take her hand and crouch beside her, trying to remain calm.

"Hey, hey, you're all right. Don't you worry. Paramedics are on their way."

She lets me hold her hand and looks into my face with confusion. "Who…?"

"I'm Logan," I explain. "Don't worry about a thing. You're going to be okay."

There's a sudden knock at the door, which is still open. The paramedics announce themselves, and I wave them in. I release Birdie's hand just as Mia comes barreling down the stairs with a stuffed giraffe in her arms.

When she sees the paramedics, she flies toward them, tears flowing anew. "Please help my mama," she cries.

One of the paramedics glares at me, which sets my teeth on edge. "Can you give us some space?"

I nod. "Mia, come here, honey. Let's let the paramedics do their thing."

She looks at me reluctantly but then joins me on the couch. We sit quietly beside each other while the paramedics start assessing Bridget. I realize Mia's watching every move they make, and I think the last thing the kid needs is to see that.

"Hey," I say, trying to distract her. I tap the giraffe's head. "Who's this guy?"

She turns a little to face me. "Gavin," she says.

"Gavin," I repeat, a little surprised. "That's a fancy name for a giraffe."

I rack my brain for something to say to this kid, something to drown out the sounds of what they are asking Bridget and their obvious concern.

"Hey," I say again. "So, do you know why the giraffe never gets invited to the other animals' parties?"

She shakes her head.

"Because he's a pain in the neck," I say and give her a smile.

She looks at me for a minute, but then it's like the joke hits her all at once and she giggles.

"Not Gavin over here, though," I say. "I'm sure he has lots of friends."

She's smiling now, which is just the calm I need for what happens next. There's a sharp knock on the door. Two uniformed police officers are peering inside. And they are looking at the bleeding woman on the floor. And then, they're looking right at me.

4

CROW

My stomach rolls over, and I immediately break out in a fresh sweat.

"So, what happened here today?" The cops are oh-so casual, but my heart's rocketing through my chest. I'm debating what to say, when the little kid jumps in and surprises the shit out of me.

She gets up off the couch and walks right up to the officer. It occurs to me this kid hasn't been taught to fear the police. She's likely never had reason to.

I look down at my hands, every instinct inside telling me to just keep it cool. There's nothing to fear here. I did nothing wrong. I don't even know these people, and I'm going to leave as soon as they take Bridget away.

"My mom fell down the stairs and got hurt," Mia explains, still gripping Gavin tightly. "I know how to dial 9-1-1, but I couldn't find her phone. She dropped it when she fell."

One of the officers is looking at me, and the other is kneeling down to focus on Mia. "Are you hurt, sweetheart?" he asks.

Everything inside me is screaming. I should never have stopped. I should never have gotten involved. This bullshit instinct inside me to help, to run in, has already been my undoing once. The officers split up, one taking Mia aside, while the other heads over to chat me up.

"Tough morning, huh?" The second officer is acting casual, but he's looking me over in a way I'm all too familiar with.

I hold my head firm. "For Bridget, unfortunately, yeah," I say, trying to deflect his attention back on her.

They're clearly assessing me while they assess the scene overall. I'm not going to make it easy for them to come to the wrong conclusion.

"Is Mia okay?" I ask, nodding at the little girl.

She's crying again and talking fast to the officer.

"I'm sure she'll be fine," the second officer says. "What's your name, sir?"

And here we go. The questioning.

"Logan Taylor," I say.

"And do you live here, Logan?" he asks.

I shake my head. "No, sir."

"Can you tell me what happened this morning?"

"Mama!" Mia cries out again when the paramedics roll a stretcher into the house.

"Excuse me," I say to the officer. I half expect him to grab me, but I'm a free man now, a private citizen, and he just lets me go up to the little girl.

I bend down and meet her eyes. "Hey, Mia." I tap Gavin's head with two fingers. "Gavin's feeling pretty nervous about the ride in the ambulance. You think you can tell him it's going to be okay? He looks like a brave giraffe, but he could use his best girl right now."

Mia nods and clutches Gavin tightly. I keep her focused on me while they get Bridget settled on the gurney.

She's a lot more alert now and is able to talk and answer questions. Once she's sitting up, she points to Mia. "My daughter," she says.

"Mama, I want to go with you."

Bridget's words don't make much sense. She's slurring a little but clearly trying hard to answer.

"You two can follow us," the paramedic says. "We need to go." He tells me the hospital he's heading to and instructs me where to park.

"I…I don't have a car here." I try to explain, but Mia hands me her mother's purse and keys.

The cops walk up to us and intervene. "You want to ride with us, honey? We can take you in the police car."

She looks from them to me, and for a minute, I'm

torn between desperately wanting her to go with them and realizing that if she does, I'm likely to end up right beside her. In the back of a cruiser. My throat feels like it's closing up. My shoulders drop as I feel a small hand on my sleeve.

"Can you drive my mom's car? I'm not allowed in a car without my car seat."

I look into those wide eyes with wonder. This is a smart kid. A kid who's been trained to be smart. She trusts the police and authority figures, knows how to dial 9-1-1. I start to suspect there's more to their story, but the cops are looking at me, waiting for my answer.

"Absolutely," I tell Mia. "You got shoes? Let's go."

The police officer who was talking to me bends down to meet Mia's eyes. "You want to ride with him, honey? Is this your mom's boyfriend?"

I don't know how the guy concluded I'm not Mia's dad, but I don't care. I hold my tongue and thank my lucky freaking stars when the kid says, "He helped me and my mom. I want to ride with him."

I have no idea why she feels that way, but I'm not about to question it. Thankfully, neither are the police. But they do leave me with a warning about meeting me at the hospital for an official statement about what happened.

I know how this has to look. Like I'm some asshole in her life who hit her or pushed her. Whatever they believe or suspect, for now, they are letting me drive the kid to the hospital.

The cops are watching our every move, and I have no clue where my phone is. I don't even know which car is hers. I call out to her, "Mia, why don't you meet me at the car? I need to grab my phone."

She runs up to me and holds out her little hand. "I put it in my pocket."

I'm impressed that tiny dress has pockets, but I don't much care as long as I'm reunited with my phone. "Great job, kiddo." I nod at her and grab Bridget's purse. Then I follow the cops and paramedics out, locking the door behind us using her keys.

Mia is standing by the beat-up red sedan parked right out front. The same one I was using as my land-mark earlier. She's waiting by the back seat, and I can see through the window there's a kid's car seat back there.

"You still ride in that thing?" I ask quietly. "How come?"

"It's the law," she explains, and I almost smile.

"Yeah?" I unlock the car and open the door for her. The ambulance is already pulling away from the house, but the uniformed officers are waiting until we take off. I groan and try to still the thundering of my heart in my chest. I'll bet any money they follow us all the way to the hospital.

Mia climbs into the seat, handing me Gavin while she fastens the belt. "I either have to turn eight or weigh forty pounds," she explains. She sounds like she's repeating the answer to a question she's asked her mom a hundred times. Then she holds out her hand for Gavin. "I turn eight in a few months."

"All right, then. You know how to do that, right?" I ask quietly. "You're all belted in?"

She nods. "I do it all the time. Mom just checks to make sure I did it."

I look at Gavin. "Gav, can I trust you to check on Mia's seat belt? I'm not an expert, but I bet you are."

Mia grins huge, and it's such a relief after all the tears, the tightness in my chest eases a little at the sight.

I climb in and immediately adjust the mirrors and move the seat as far back as it will go. The low fuel light goes on the moment I turn the key, and I curse softly under my breath.

I have no clue how much gas in is here, but the hospital we're going to is only a few miles away. I'm going to press my luck yet again and hope the guardian angels of good deeds look kindly on me for once.

Just as I turn over the engine, my phone rings.

"Goddamn…" I look up at the kid in the back seat, and I hold back the rest of my curses. The caller ID is Arrow, probably wanting to know why I didn't respond to his text earlier. I swipe the screen and bark out, "Hey, Arrow, man, now's not the best time."

He's saying hello and starts talking, but just then, I see the blue and red lights on the cruiser behind me turn on.

"I'll call you later," I tell him and toss my phone in the passenger seat.

"Are you okay?" Mia asks from the back. "What's your name again? I kind of forgot."

"I am, sweetheart," I say. "You can call me Crow."

"Crow?" she asks. "That's not your real name, is it?"

I meet her eyes in the rearview. She looks amused. Interested.

"No, it's a nickname," I tell her. "Didn't you tell me your mom's name is Bridget, but people call her Birdie?"

Mia's eyes open like I've just unlocked a treasure chest of toys in front of her. "No way," she blurts. "Crow is a bird, and my mom's nickname is also about a bird. That's crazy."

"If you want, you can call me Logan."

"Logan kind of rhymes with Gavin," she says, clutching her giraffe.

"It kind of does," I agree, but it so doesn't.

"I like both," she says. "Logan and Crow. Can I call you both? Like I sometimes say Mom but mostly call her Mama?"

I nod. "That works, kiddo. Do you have a nickname?"

She smiles. "My mom calls me sweetie and honey, but those aren't really nicknames. She just says that because she loves me." She's quiet for a moment and then says, "You just called me kiddo. My dad calls me kiddo sometimes. Is that a nickname?"

"Sort of," I say, distracted. Since she's brought up the issue of a dad, I latch on to that. "Mia, do you know how to reach your dad?"

She nods. "His number is in my mom's phone."

Well, for fuck's sake. Of course it is. And her mom's phone is some place in their house.

"Is your daddy at work? Is he coming back home tonight? Someone should find a way to let him know what's going on with you and your mom."

Mia shakes her head. "I don't know where he works. He's never lived in the house with us." She seems totally casual as she adds, "I only see him once in a while. It's been a long time. I don't think Mama would want me to call him unless it was a real emergency. But this is an emergency, isn't it?"

She looks ready to start crying again, so I redirect the conversation. "Do you have any grandparents? Brothers or sisters? Anyone else your mom calls when she needs help?"

Mia's lower lip starts to tremble, and I immediately regret asking the question.

"There was just my grandma," she starts. "She's in heaven now. There's no one else."

Double fuck.

"That's okay," I assure her. "No problem. How about school, honey? Where do you go to school? Do you ever have a babysitter come watch you?"

I assume the school will have a list of emergency contacts. There's got to be someone I can notify that Bridget is hurt and Mia is going to need care.

"My friends Sophia or Kylee…their moms watch me sometimes if Mom's going to be late picking me up from afterschool," she says.

I have no idea what afterschool is, but I roll with it. "Okay, that's great. Sophia and Kylee, you said?" Helpful moms are great news for me if I can find this Kylee or this Sophia and one of their moms. "And your school?"

She tells me the name of a local elementary school, a place I've never heard of, because of course, why would I? I've never spent this much time with a kid, let alone been anywhere near a school. At least not since I was a student in one myself.

I flip on the radio and let some pop music play for the few minutes while I follow the ambulance and police cruiser as best as I can without breaking every traffic law.

I breathe a sigh of relief as soon as we hit the hospital parking lot. "All right, Mia. We're here." I go around to the passenger side and help the kid out of the back. "You forgot something," I remind her.

Gavin the giraffe is lying facedown on the floor. Mia grins at me and shakes her head. "That would have been a pain in the neck," she says, chuckling.

I crack a half smile. "Hey," I say. "Good joke. You remembered."

She looks at me awkwardly, as if I'm supposed to take her hand or something. We are in a parking lot after all, and even though she's, like, a sort of big kid, I don't know what the rules are. I hold out my hand tentatively, and when she grabs it firmly, I guess I did the right thing. Whether it feels right or not is another thing. But whether I'm doing this right or doing this wrong isn't something I'm going to worry about right now. Mia, and Gavin, for that matter, are looking up at me—the only grown-up around—and they are waiting for me to do something.

"Let's find your mom," I say, and I walk her through the parking lot toward the emergency department.

As we walk into the hospital, I realize I forgot her last name. "Mia, what's your last name?"

"Connor," she says. "Same as Mama's."

"And your dad?" I ask.

"Mama and my dad never got married, so he has a different last name. Bryan Harris."

Her answer is so polished, so well-rehearsed.

We walk into the emergency room, and it's a lot less busy than I would expect for this hour of the morning. Mia and I head up to the registration desk, and before I have the chance to open my mouth, Mia starts in.

"Can I please see my mom?" Her lip is trembling, but she's got a firm, clear, big-girl voice on.

Hearing her sound so brave, I feel like a little fist clenches around my heart. I can't imagine how scary this is for her, and yet here she is, asking loudly and politely all the right questions.

The triage nurse looks like she feels the same way, her eyes going soft. She cocks her head to the side and directs all her questions to Mia.

"All right, sweetheart. Let me get some information. What's your mother's name?"

Mia and the nurse talk, and with a few taps on her keyboard, the nurse nods at me. "Sir, may I get your name?"

I give it to her, and she motions for us to take a seat.

"I'll have someone come out and bring you to your mama as soon as I can, sweetie."

As easy as that, we're sitting together, me, Mia, and Gavin. And oddly, it doesn't feel terrible. I'm uncomfortable about the cops, but if not for them, I have nowhere else to be. And the thought of leaving Mia alone and not knowing that Birdie is safe and on her way home… I lean back in the chair and wait.

Mia swings her legs and asks me questions about my tattoos. The birds I have inked on my flesh. Typical old-school sparrows, with red breasts and black wings. The inkwork is simple but still perfect after all these years. I can't count the times I looked at those birds while I was in prison, wishing I could spread my wings and fly away.

I tell her the story of where I got them, leaving out the R-rated details, since the truth is, the sparrows were a gift from a stripper I dated about a decade ago who worked days as a tattoo apprentice.

We're sitting in the chairs, shooting the shit with ease as if we've known each other for years instead of just hours. For a second, I think about what Morris must have gone through meeting Alice and Zoey. He saw a woman in need and stepped right up to help her. Zoey was right there, and they snagged Morris, hook, line, and sinker.

When the nurse calls Mia's name and she jumps off the chair and takes my hand, I realize how easy it would be to become attached.

5

BRIDGET

"Really, I'm fine... I just need to see my daughter. Can anyone tell me if my daughter is here?"

I am so, so far from fine. I'm about a minute away from total mom freak-out mode.

I have no idea where my daughter is. I missed the biggest meeting of my career so far, and there is no way I am going to have a job tomorrow.

But after getting stitches in my eyebrow and being taken for a bunch of tests, I'm feeling more alert. More like myself. The entire staff at the hospital are treating me like something is seriously, seriously wrong, when really, all I care about is what's happening with Mia.

After I answer the same questions over and over again, a nurse tells me they're considering admitting me, and that's when I literally start to lose it.

"No." I shake my head, but that small movement

triggers a blast of pain. "I can't be admitted. I have no childcare. Please," I beg, hoping the nurse will pass along my concerns to whoever is in charge of my treatment. They keep referring to doctors and radiologists and all these other people who are making decisions about my future. But the nurse at the bedside in the ER room they've got me in has been so, so kind. She listens and seems genuinely sympathetic when I talk about insurance and out-of-pocket expenses. "Can't I just get a referral and see a doctor later this week?"

The nurse gives me another kind smile. "We'll see what the doctor says."

I don't like the sound of that. Not one bit. But before I can argue, the curtain in the cubicle I've been placed in moves aside, and I hear a voice that brings tears to my eyes.

"Mama!" Mia is throwing herself at me, climbing up onto the bed to hold me.

I don't care how much it hurts, I close my eyes and grip my daughter to my chest. I stroke her hair, the ballerina bun I put in this morning now messy and falling to one side. The tears flow down my face so fast, I can't stop them.

"Baby. My baby." I rock back and forth just a bit, clutching my sweet girl as hard as my weak arms will allow. "I'm so sorry. You must have been so scared. Are you okay?"

We're both crying so hard and talking over each other that I hardly notice the man standing a few feet away. He's beside the parted curtain, and while he looks like he doesn't want to come too close, he's looking right at me.

He's got a haunted, dark look about him. His long night-black hair is slightly messed up, and he's got a dark beard across his chin and jaw. He's wearing an armband around his bicep, which is hilarious, because the man's so big and tattooed, he looks like with one flex, he could snap the phone holster right off his arm. While he's imposing and dark, he's holding Gavin the giraffe between his hands and looking completely out of place.

"Excuse me?" I call out and then motion him to come closer. I recognize his face as the man from my house. I untangle one arm from my grip on Mia and extend my hand. "I'm Birdie," I say. "Are you the man who helped us this morning?"

He nods and shifts Gavin to his other hand, and he awkwardly slings my purse over one shoulder. Then he reaches out his hand to shake mine. His grip is warm and firm, but he releases me quickly. "I'm Logan."

Mia steps in to fill in the gaps. "Logan drove me here. He tells great jokes. Also, Mama, his nickname is Crow. Just like your nickname is Birdie, he has a bird nickname."

Crow? The man's nickname is Crow? And he drove my daughter here? While I'm panicked a man I don't know has had custody of my daughter for the last few hours, I'm also incredibly grateful to this Crow person.

Mia seems fine—better than I would expect, even—and I can't imagine a better endorsement at the moment than a man who tells great jokes.

"Birdie," he says, his voice low. "How are you feeling?"

I sigh. "That's the million-dollar question. Meaning they want to run a million tests before they'll tell me."

I debate briefly whether I should say more. I don't owe this man an explanation, but he is my knight in shining armor, so I feel like I owe him at least a little detail.

"I get migraines sometimes," I say, "and lately, I've had some issues. It came on really strong this morning. I was trying to get downstairs to get some medicine, and I tripped over that damn loose carpet on the stairs. At least, I think that's what happened." I look at Mia and mumble, "Sorry, I shouldn't have said damn."

Logan twists his lips into an almost smile.

"It's okay, Mama. You've had a hard morning."

I look into my daughter's eyes and just lose it. Yes, I have had a hard morning. But I've also had a hard month. A hard year. Everything lately has been hard. If a pink slip is waiting for me on my desk, things are about to get so much harder. And I am already so, so tired. I can't imagine things getting worse. The realization that they may, that they *will,* sends me into a moment of panic. I hold my daughter closer, and I can't stop the tears.

Before I realize what I started, Mia's crying, and Logan's looking at Gavin in his hands like he doesn't know where he belongs in all this. He steps closer to my bed and grabs the box of tissues from the side table. After he pulls three from the box, he hands two to me and takes one and starts pretending to dab Gavin's eyes.

"Lot of tears in here today, Gav," he says, talking to the stuffed giraffe. "You going be all right, little buddy?"

Mia immediately pivots from tears to giggles. She holds her hand out for Gav. Logan hands over the stuffed animal, and Mia holds him close. "You're going to be okay, little buddy," she says very, very quietly under her breath to her toy.

She hasn't played with stuffed animals or talked to them in a very long time.

"Gav," I say, "I know you can be brave. You've already been a very brave little guy." I smooth Mia's hair and take a few deep breaths to calm my emotions. "We're going to be okay," I whisper. "We all will."

Crow is staring at us, and I start to apologize.

"Logan, I'm so sorry. I'm sure you had places to be today..."

He holds up a hand. "That's all right." He sets my purse on the table next to the box of tissues. "I'm free today. Was happy to help. Are they going to release you, you think?"

I shrug. "I hope so. They're waiting for the results of one of the tests to make sure I don't have..." I pause, not wanting to say too much in front of Mia. "... anything going on. Once that's back, I'm hoping they will let me go. I just want to go home and rest in my own bed. Put this whole day behind me." I look at the man, so huge in this small space that he looks like he hardly fits. He's hunching his shoulders, and I notice he's wearing running clothes. "Logan, I...I don't know how to thank you. You drove Mia here? How did you even know to come help?"

"I was running by, and Mia asked to use my phone to call 9-1-1. She was a real champ. Your phone seems to be missing, but she was able to find your keys and purse, so I drove her here. The police offered to bring her, but she wanted to ride in the car so you'd have a way home. And so she could ride in her seat thing there." He nods, and a flush of embarrassment heats my cheeks.

I was almost out of gas, and the car was probably a mess. I don't know how he even fit in my small sedan.

The man's legs look like tree trunks stuffed into gray sweatpants.

"Mia was a real hero," he says, nodding at her. He's so serious, but there's a lightness that comes through the dark exterior. "I just followed her lead. She knew exactly what to do."

"What happened after I fell down the stairs, baby?" I stroke Mia's hair, desperately wanting to fill in the gaps. I have vague memories. I know I lost consciousness for a bit, but mostly, I remember being scared and in pain and feeling like if I moved, I'd get sick.

"I couldn't find your phone, so I went outside. I knocked on the house next door, but no one answered."

Oh God. My heart lodges in my throat as I picture my baby, her tiny fist pounding on a neighbor's door for help. How scared she must have been.

"Then Crow ran by and stopped." Mia points to Logan and gives him a smile. "Although if he was really a crow, he would have been flying." She giggles. "And you know the rest, Mama."

I don't, though. I don't know the rest, and I want to. Want to know every second of what happened when this man stepped into my house, swooping in to save the day.

"I don't know how I can repay you," I say. "I'd like to try. Can I get your contact information? Buy you dinner or... I don't know, Logan. Crow." As I start to get stressed out thinking about what comes next, everything just hurts. My face, my head. My heart. I rest my chin against Mia's head and close my eyes. "I would take your contact information, but like you said, I have no clue where my phone is. I was at the top of the stairs talking to my boss when I dropped it."

He shakes his head. "You don't owe me anything."

I stop him with a hand. "Please," I say. "My God, you've done so much. I insist."

His dark eyes grow more intense as he looks at me, his full lips set in a serious frown. Not a frown, exactly, but when I look past the sexy stubble, his mouth is tight. Like he's uncomfortable. And the poor man probably is.

"I...I have my own debts to repay. I was happy to help. Don't worry about it."

His own debts to repay...

I watch the attractive stranger and try to make sense of his words. But before I can think it through, there's a sudden sound of footsteps outside my little partition.

"Ms. Connor?" The nurse pops her head past the curtain. She looks from Mia to Logan. "There are a couple officers here. They'd like to ask you a few questions if you're feeling up to it."

"The police?" I'm confused. Why on earth would the police show up here with questions?

Logan's lips tighten into a very decisive frown now. He nods at me. "A woman with an injury and a man on the scene." He rubs the stubble on his chin with a hand. "Doesn't look good."

With those three words, I understand.

"I'm fine to talk to them," I tell the nurse with a smile. "Thank you."

The officers step through the curtain and look from Logan to Mia to me.

"Ms. Connor?" the younger of the two talks to me, while the older man stands beside Logan. "How are you feeling?"

I give them a weak smile and meet the officer's eyes. "I'm so much better now. Thank you." I motion to Logan. "Logan, would you mind taking Mia to the cafeteria for something to eat?" I kiss my daughter's hair. "I'll bet she's starving."

Mia nods and gives me a hug before scooting to the edge of the bed. Logan reaches out a hand to her, and she takes it without hesitation. He helps her jump down from the bed, and then, Gavin in one hand and my daughter's in the other, he looks away from the cops.

"Logan, take my purse. You can use my debit card. I don't think I have any cash." I mentally calculate the balance in my account, but unless Logan buys Mia everything in the cafeteria, I should have enough in there to cover it. "And of course, please get yourself whatever you need. You've got to be starving."

He shakes his head. "I've got it covered. We'll be back later."

As this stranger takes my daughter away yet again, I rest my head back against the pillows. I'm so, so tired. There is no reason I should trust this man with Mia, and yet, I feel a lot more concerned about why the police are here.

"Ms. Connor." The officer points to my forehead. "Looks like you have a pretty nasty cut there. Do you remember how it happened?"

I give the officers another smile. They are just doing their job. I try to remind myself that if I were a victim of violence, I'd need them to do exactly what they are here to do right now. Following up. Confirming. Making sure I am safe.

"I do remember," I say. "I've been having headaches lately. One came on really fast this morning, and I tripped over some loose carpeting on the stairs. I've been meaning to fix it, but…I've been meaning to get to a lot of things."

They ask me a few more questions. About Logan, how long I've known him, and whether he was in my house any time before the 9-1-1 call. On some level, I appreciate that these men are doing a job. But right now, I'm exhausted. I'm sure there are women out there who need this kind of intervention, but that's not the case here.

"Can I give you a business card?" the officer asks after I answer all their questions. "If you need support, the county has some services."

I don't hesitate before answering. "Sure, of course. Thank you."

They hand me a business card. It's got a sunshine logo on it and has a toll-free number I can call for information about county programs. But since there's no crime, there's no problem. And nothing more for the officers to do here.

"Best of luck with your headaches, ma'am." They look me over one last time and then head out.

When I'm finally alone, I lay my head back against the pillows and close my eyes. I have no clue who I'm going to call or how I'm going to manage the mess I've made of today.

When the curtain moves aside and Mia and Logan come back, I'm surprised at the relief I feel looking at their faces.

Logan's chin is set, and his dark eyes flash. "Everything all right here?"

I understand what he's asking, and I nod. "Yeah," I sigh. "They left."

The doctor comes in then, and the tiny space is suddenly very crowded. Logan steps aside but stays close to the curtain. Mia climbs back into my lap.

"So, I have some good news." The doctor explains

that I have a mild concussion from the fall. "That was a decent tumble you took," he says. "The cut on your face is likely to swell, and don't be surprised if you get a black eye and some bruising, but there's nothing on the initial scan to suggest a serious brain injury."

When he says brain injury, I look at Mia, but she doesn't look afraid. She looks tired and is resting her head against the front of my hospital gown.

"Do you have help at home?" The doctor looks from Logan to me. He doesn't wait for me to answer and starts explaining post-concussion care. What I should do, what I shouldn't. He hands me a bunch of paperwork so I can follow up with some other doctors this week, but the real kicker comes when he says at the end, "Since we don't know how exactly the fall happened, I'm tempted to medically restrict you from driving."

No driving?

"What?" I ask. "Why? For how long?"

He hands me a fact sheet about concussions and recovery. "I recommend you take a week to ten days to recover. No strenuous activity, no driving. If you can get into a specialist in the next two weeks, that doctor will want to run tests and can better assess how you're recovering. That should provide a clearer idea of the timeline for a return to normal levels of activity."

I lower my chin and say nothing. A week to ten days? And then maybe longer? I feel the sting of defeated tears burn my eyes. The fall, the fear, the pain, the costs… That would have been enough. But now this? Everything about my whole life is going to be disrupted. Making things even harder for both me and my child. Harder is something I literally cannot afford. Disruption is something I'm not prepared to work around.

My lower lip trembles, and I bite it to try to keep myself calm. The doctor is talking about symptoms, what to look out for over the next few days, but I can't listen. Can't focus.

"Bridget, do you have a ride home?" The doctor must have asked this already because the silence in the room as he waits for my answer feels heavy. Like he's weighing whether I'm ready to go home based on how well I understand him.

Before I have the chance to say a word, Logan speaks up.

"Yeah. I'm driving her." His stare on me is intense, searching. I can't say for sure why being the center of this man's attention isn't unnerving. There's kindness and sadness behind Logan's very guarded expression. "I'll take care of everything," he says.

He can't. I know he can't. I don't even know what he means by that. He's a stranger.

But as I study him, I think through what he's done today alone. He's held my purse, my daughter's hand,

and Gavin the giraffe. Tears sting my eyes, and I think about calling everyone in my phone book, even Mia's dad, but without my phone…I'll never remember anyone's number. I'm fully fucked. Without options. Helpless. And that feeling crushes me.

As if picking up on my struggle, Logan looks at me, his brows knitted together in worry.

I shake my head and start to resist, but just then, Mia drops Gavin on the floor, and Logan bends down to pick up the plush toy. When he does, he lifts Gav and brushes him off, removing nonexistent dust from the floor.

"This guy might need a bath later," Logan says, his voice soft. "He keeps ending up on the floor."

Mia giggles and takes the toy back.

I swallow hard, and I search the faces of the men in the room—the doctor, who has no clue what anxiety his words are causing. And this other man. The one who's given up almost a whole day of his life for a stranger in need. My mom is gone; Mia's dad's not here. I struggle to accept the feeling I've been fighting for months now —defeat. But I'm there. Out of options. And the one ray of light in my world is a dark, handsome man who looks like he's carrying burdens of his own.

I should say no. Should refuse his help. I can never repay it. I know that. Whether it's money or time or something else he'll want in return, I know I won't have it. I have nothing to give anyone.

"Thank you, Logan," I say quietly, squeezing Mia tight.

This is just a ride. That's it. I'm going to let him take me as far as the front door of my house. Once I close the door and get back inside, I'll be alone again. I promise myself that I'll repay him for his kindness and help, and I'll do whatever it takes to keep myself and Mia afloat.

6

CROW

THE DRIVE BACK TO BRIDGET'S HOUSE IS A LOT MORE awkward than I expect. Mia chatters away about school and dinner, while Bridget listens beside me in the front seat. I can tell her mind is racing. She's twisting a business card in her hands, tearing at the edges with her nails. The tension she's giving off can't be good for her head.

"That from the cops?" I ask quietly, ticking my chin at her hands.

She nods, and I hear something pained in her voice as she says, "County services. In case I need them."

I pull into a cheap gas station not far from the hospital. Bridget tries to shove her debit card at me. I ignore her and turn to get out, but she stops me with a hand on my arm.

Her hand on me is firm and warm, surprisingly

strong after what she's been through today. Her face is starting to bruise and swell from the stitches, and her color isn't great. She needs some food and some real rest, but when she touches me, I get lost for a moment in the sensation.

"Logan," she says, her voice soft. "You've done so much. I can pay for the gas."

"How about this," I say. "You stop trying to fight me and rest."

Bridget looks confused. "And if I do? You'll let me pay for the gas?"

I smile. "No. But you might as well save your energy and stop fighting me since you're going to lose either way." I look down at her slim fingers lightly pressing against the inked birds on my arm. I pull away from her touch and immediately miss the contact.

"Relax," I tell her. "I'm just going to put a couple bucks in the tank."

I don't want any more hurt for Birdie. Whether I know her or not, I recognize the struggle in her eyes. The defeat. And if I can take a little bit of that away from her by just doing what I can, then I'm going to. It's a lot more than I can do for myself.

Despite driving on empty, Bridget's car has been fairly well maintained. I make a note to pop the hood when we get back to her place, but then I remember the stairs and the missing phone. There's a lot more to do than giving her car an inspection.

I start making lists in my head and recognize an unfamiliar feeling in my chest. It's new, and it drives me forward, like an invisible thread that I can follow from one moment to the next.

Maybe it's a weird form of power. Maybe it's hope. All I know is, for the first time in a damn long time, I like the way things feel. I'm sweaty and hungry and would really like to get out of these funky running shoes, but having Bridget in the car, her eyes following my every move, and Mia in the back, a little bit more of that sadness gone from her face... This feels a lot like living. Like life.

It's nothing I've felt in years.

And it feels good.

I give the hood an approving tap and then climb in behind the wheel. "Car's in good shape," I say. "I only had enough cash on me for a couple gallons, but it'll get us home."

Birdie's eyes are half closed, but she smiles when she thanks me. "Are you a mechanic?" she asks. "The only way my luck could get better today is if you told me you were a headache specialist."

"I cause more headaches than I cure," I say, a half grin on my lips. "But yeah, I work with these." I crack my knuckles and then start up the car and head back toward Bridget's house. "Cars, houses, small engines. If it's mechanical, I can probably get it going. Electronics —phones, computers...not so much."

Her eyes are fully closed now, and I notice that Mia has dozed off in the warmth of the late afternoon. The sunlight hits her face, and I watch the rays move from her to her stuffed toy as I drive.

Mia seems to relax more the farther we get from the hospital, and I do the same. The tension in my shoulders sags, and suddenly, I'm tired too. Exhausted.

When we arrive at the house, I pull the car into the exact spot it was parked this morning, right outside at the curb. I hurry around to the passenger side and help Bridget out. I offer her my hand, and at first, she refuses.

"I'm okay," she says. "I can do it."

But then she reaches for the strap of her purse and moans slightly as she angles the strap over her shoulder.

"Okay," she chuckles, holding out her hand. "I'm not going to be a hero."

I take her hand, and she looks from our hands clasped tightly palm-to-palm and carefully steps onto the sidewalk.

"Thank you," she says, her voice tight.

"Got your keys?" I ask.

She unzips her bag and digs through it while I open

the back door and unfasten Mia's seat belt. She wakes up as I snap the buckle a little loudly.

"Sorry to wake you," I mutter. "But we're home, Mia."

She yawns and then gives me a sleepy grin before handing Gavin to me while she climbs out of the back.

Bridget locks the car, and the three of us walk to the front door, a ragtag, worn-out group. It's been a day, but walking up to the house feels somehow familiar. Right. And that fucking scares me.

Once Bridget unlocks that door, my reason for being here will end. That sneaks up on me like a wildfire, and I feel a sudden dread replace the momentary good feelings. Somehow dread feels easier, more familiar.

I let it take over. I don't belong here. I'm just the good Samaritan. The ride home. All the light and hope of just a few minutes ago start seeping away.

Bridget's hand is shaky as she jingles her keys and puts the house key into the lock. She doesn't seem like she should be alone just yet. But what am I going to do? Leave Mia and Bridget to fend for themselves all night?

Yes, I tell myself. That's exactly what I have to do. This may have been the best day of the last few years for me, but this has been a horrible one for Bridget and Mia. I'm sure they just want to put all this behind them. Including me.

Bridget opens the door, and Mia runs inside. She

races ahead to use the bathroom, leaving her mother and me alone.

"Home sweet home," she sighs. She walks in, but I stay planted on the front stoop. "Logan?" She's looking at me, the bruising that's darkening her face making her look even more vulnerable and tired. "Aren't you coming in?"

"Uh…I can," I say.

She shakes her head. "No, I'm sorry. I don't know what's wrong with me. It's okay. You've given up your whole day for us. I don't want to keep you." She walks into the kitchen and grabs a pad of paper and pen from a basket and then comes back to the front door. "Can I get your contact information? I'd really like to be able to get in touch once I find my phone."

Shit, her phone.

"Let me help you find it," I say, stepping inside. "It's not safe to leave you like this without any way to call if you need something."

I stand there just inside the doorway, and it's as if by walking into her house, invited and wanted even for just a little bit, I'd be taking a major step forward into my future.

"Would you mind?" She drops her arms to her sides, looking exhausted. "If I have to crawl around on my hands and knees to find it…"

And just like that, I step inside.

"Logan, can I offer you water or tea or something? I've got sweet tea made."

"Some sweet tea would be great." I look up at the stairs and spot that loose bit of carpeting. I trace the path a phone could have gone if she dropped it from the top of the stairs.

If the phone hit the tile and skidded, it's got to be some place. I crawl around on my hands and knees, reaching under furniture and find it almost immediately.

"Got it." I pull the device out from under a small bookshelf. It was far enough back there that Mia's little arms would never have reached it even if she did know it was under there. "Screen's not even cracked."

"Well, at least the day isn't complete shit." Bridget takes the device from me and hands me a tall glass filled with ice and a light-colored tea drink. "Thank you so much," she says. She stifles a yawn. "I don't know how I'll ever repay you. For all of this."

"Thanks for the tea," I say. "Now, just a couple things before I get going." I point at the stairs. "You mind if I take a look at that carpet?"

She shakes her head, and I go up just as Mia runs up the stairs. She meets me at the top, Gavin still in her hands.

"Whatcha doing?" she asks, dropping onto the top step and sitting down. She watches as I sit on the stair with the loose carpet.

"See here?" I ask, pointing to the carpet. "I'm going to take a look at what's underneath here. If you have nice floors, I might be able to get rid of this old carpeting for you completely." I meet Mia's eyes and give her a look. "No more tripping." I tug at the loose piece, moving it carefully so I can see how it was applied and what condition the floor is underneath. "Oh yeah. We're in luck. The carpet is covering up a really nice floor." I'm saying it loudly and looking down at Bridget now. "When your mom's feeling better, maybe I'll pull up this carpeting and clean up these floors. In the meantime, I don't have tools or anything with me to repair this." I look at Bridget. "Can you sleep down here for a night or two? I can get back tomorrow with tools."

The look on her face is unreadable at first, but then she starts to sputter. "Logan, I can't let you do that."

I nod and hand Mia the still-damp towel that's been sitting on the carpet since Birdie's fall this morning. "Honey, can you put this some place for your mom?"

She grabs the towel from my hands and dashes off.

"You've raised a smart kid."

Birdie's response is proud but tinged with sadness. "She's had to be."

Mia returns from wherever she took that towel and sits back on the top step. "So, now what?" she asks.

"Honey, now nothing. We need to let Logan go home. He's given up his whole day taking care of us."

I head back down the stairs, stopping beside Birdie in the foyer. "Just watch the loose spot," I say. "Consider putting up a handrail on the wall."

Mia follows me down and cocks her head at her mom. "Why can't he fix it, Mama? He said the floor is good."

"Honey, it's…it's complicated."

Bridget stands beside me at the bottom of the stairs, and for the first time, I stare directly into her eyes. They're a cloudy gray, like the sky during the most perfect rain. She draws her lower lip between her teeth and exhales deeply through her nose.

"Anything else I can do before I head out?"

I check the time on my phone. It's almost six. If I head out now, I'll make it back to the compound before dark. I'm starving, so I won't have the energy to run, which means I'll be walking.

"Would you at least stay for dinner?" Bridget's face looks as tired as I feel. "Pizza? I'm not much of a cook."

I bite back a grin, thinking about the sweet tea, and I nod. "Pizza would be great."

Mia starts to clap as she plops down on the couch and turns on the TV. "Mama, am I going to school tomorrow?"

"Honey, I don't…I don't know. Let's just have some dinner, and we'll figure everything out."

She punches a number on her phone and asks me

what I like on my pizza.

"Your call," I say. "Unless you like weird shit." I flick a look at Mia.

"What qualifies as weird?" Bridget asks.

"Pineapple," I say. "Anything else..." I put my fingers to my lips and make a kissing sound. "Delish."

Her smile eases a little of the pain in her face, and she places the order. Mia is sitting on the couch, absorbed in some cartoon and cuddling Gavin. Kids are so resilient. So strong. After a long and exhausting day, Mia seems totally fine. She just let the day go. It's Bridget and I who both look like we're carrying suitcases full of bricks up a steep hill.

"Can I see your phone?" I ask.

She hands over the device, and I enter my contact info. "Now you know how to reach me," I say.

She looks at my name and smiles. "Logan Taylor. That's such a pretty name for such a..." She stops herself.

I chuckle. "It's all right." I scrub a hand over my face. "You can tell me I'm not pretty."

She laughs and motions for me to join her in the kitchen. "It's not that," she says.

I follow her into the small, open kitchen. If we talk quietly, Mia might not be able to hear us, but I like that the floor plan allows an unobstructed view of the rest of the downstairs.

"Logan," she says, dropping into a chair. She motions for me to sit. "I have to be honest with you." She rests her face in her hands. "I'm...I'm at a loss for how to repay you. Pizza doesn't begin to cut it. You spent an entire workday taking care of my kid... I would love nothing more than to hire you to fix my stairs. If I had the extra funds, I would have fixed them already." She laces her fingers together and stares down at her hands. "Mia's dad isn't in the picture, never has been, so there's no support there, if you know what I mean. He sees her, and they have more of a fun-uncle-type relationship, which is better than nothing. I try not to say anything bad about him in front of his daughter, but we're on our own. This was my mom's house, so I'm fortunate to have a roof over my head. There's just not a lot left over for extra. Like home maintenance. And doctor visits."

I watch her face as she talks, and it's not just the long years of loneliness and defeat that draw me in. Bridget is stunning. Her face is so expressive, her eyes so honest when she looks at me. Right now, she's staring into her hands as if admitting she's committed a crime. She's way too hard on herself. Handling what she has all these years is nothing to be ashamed of. She should be proud. Damn proud.

"My mom passed a while back, and the stress of managing everything all alone..." She looks up at me then, those gray eyes pooling tears like raindrops. "And of course, these headaches… That's just been the straw that's breaking this camel's back." She bites her lower lip to stop it from trembling and meets my eyes, a gentle lift to her chin.

"But I promise," she continues, "I'll repay you for this kindness, the gas money, and the food you bought Mia at the hospital. I don't like to be in debt."

In spite of myself, I reach out to her and grab her hand. It's a fast, reassuring gesture. Just my hand on hers for a second before I pull away. Her eyes flash with something—not anger, not fear, but I'm not sure exactly what it is.

"I did what I did without expecting anything in return," I say. "I know a thing or two about repaying debts. And I'm not here to make the hole you've been in feel any deeper." I pace the kitchen, putting some distance between those rain-cloud eyes and myself. "I'd like to fix the carpet for you. It could help me out, actually. I'd like to do more home remodeling work, and if I do a good job, I can use you as a reference."

I don't know where that's coming from, but all of a sudden, it feels like a good idea. A way to ease my dependence on Leo and Tim and the shop that really doesn't have enough work for me anyway. It'll be impossible to get started as a contractor on my own without tools, materials, and insurance, but maybe somebody will hire me on if I can prove I've got the skills. And having work of my own will give me a real excuse to get Arrow off my back. The pressure to work with him on shit I don't want will ease up if I'm getting other jobs.

"Really?" she asks. "You'd do that? I mean, of course I'd be happy to give you a reference. I just feel weird letting you work for free."

"I only want a reference after I've done the work," I say sternly. "And only if you're happy with the outcome. I'm not asking for any favors."

"You're doing me the favor." She smiles. "We're two sides of the same broken record, Logan."

There's a knock at the door, and she starts to stand, but I motion for her to stay. "Let me."

I check the peephole and see it's the pizza guy, so I yank open the door. I've got twenty dollars in my armband, what's left after buying Mia breakfast and putting a few bucks of gas in the tank, so I take the pizza and hand the kid the cash. "Sorry. It's all I've got on me today, man," I say. I don't really know what a good tip is anymore. This is the first time I've paid for a food delivery since I came back.

The kid waves away my cash. "It's okay, mister. You guys tipped on the app when you ordered. Thanks, though."

"You tipped on the app?" I close and lock the door and bring the pizza to Bridget in the kitchen.

She nods. "I always do. It's safer than keeping cash around the house."

When she says that, it hits me again that Bridget is a woman living all alone with a small kid. She's got a mild concussion, and I'm supposed to go home and just leave her to fend for herself all night. I don't like the feeling, yet I don't belong here. It's not my place to stay, and I think if Bridget knew about my past, she'd be hustling my ass out of here so fast, I'd be the one whose head was spinning.

I eat a couple slices of pizza and choke it back with Bridget's tea. Mia's eating on the couch with Gavin while Bridget and I talk quietly about her job. She's vague on the topic, not really wanting to talk about it, so I don't press the issue. God only knows I don't want to be pressed, and she hasn't asked anything so far that I haven't easily answered.

She finishes off a slice of pepperoni and meets my eyes. "You should take my car," she says quietly.

"Sorry?"

She wipes her mouth with a napkin, dark circles forming under her eyes. "I'm not going to work tomorrow, and I'm probably going to have to keep Mia home from school. I think we will spend a good part of the night on the couch watching TV. You shouldn't have to walk or pay for a ride after everything you've been through today. Might as well take my car. You can bring it back when you come to fix the stairs."

"Tomorrow?" I ask. "You want me to come back tomorrow?"

She meets my eyes. "If you can. I mean, if you can..."

"Tomorrow," I insist, saying it before she can backpedal. "I can do tomorrow."

After we eat, I help Bridget load the dishes in the dishwasher and head to the door. As I drive off in her car, I wave at Mia, who is using Gavin's paw to wave goodbye to me. Bridget's at the door, leaning against the jamb, just watching as I pull away.

This is literally the best day I've had in years.

When I get back to the compound, it's after eight. Tiny's in the kitchen, talking on the phone to his daughter Lia and drinking a beer. He raises a brow at me in greeting and continues his conversation. No questions about where I was all day. Just a brother greeting a brother. Trust. This is what family is to me now, and I give Tiny a good-natured punch on the shoulder as I grab a beer from the fridge and head back to my room.

After I shower, I lie between my sheets and close my eyes, and for once, something other than emptiness lulls me to sleep. It's a feeling that's dangerously close to peace.

7

BRIDGET

THE NEXT MORNING, I DRAG MYSELF UP THE STAIRS, carefully lifting my feet over each step. I leave Mia sound asleep, tucked under an afghan hand-crocheted by my mom, on the couch. I'd set the alarm to go off early but ended up waking up before it even went off...again.

I check my phone while the coffee brews, giddy when I see a text from my knight in the gray sweatpants.

Logan: *You awake? In pain?*

Me: *Yes and yeah. I'm making myself some coffee and will take something to help. My eyebrow feels like I went a couple rounds in a boxing ring. The black eye I have really fits the look.*

Logan: *Eat a few bites of food too. You don't want the pain pills sitting in an empty stomach.*

Me: *I'll choke something down.*

Logan: *Good. Be there in a bit.*

I kind of want to say that I'm looking forward to it, but that feels…inappropriate, maybe? Yeah, Logan is hot, kind, and funny, but he's basically a stranger. For all I know, he could be a serial killer, a tax evader—or, like my dad, an asshole with a whole family on the side.

I resist overthinking the whole thing. I turn on the shower, assessing every ache and pain one by one. Sore face, yes. My eyebrow throbs a bit. I'm dizzy, but nothing bad, and the stinging behind my eyes is fatigue, but nothing like yesterday. The aura and shimmering behind my eyes are gone. I may have a mild concussion, but none of the signs of an impending migraine are there.

I check the water temperature and move slowly, putting a clean towel and my robe close to the bathtub so that once I climb in, all I have to do is stand under the water. I'll be careful. I'm steady enough to shower and not fall.

Once I'm in the shower, the impulse to scrub my hair and shave my legs overtakes me, but when I bend to grab the shaving gel, a nice throb in my eyebrow reminds me I'm only here to do essential cleaning. Nothing extra. Under the hot spray, I can't help but close my eyes and replay the events of yesterday. No, that's not entirely honest.

I can't help but think about Logan.

I wonder who this mystery man really is. Why

wasn't he at work yesterday? Why he doesn't have a wife or family—although, I suppose he could. It's not as if we talked about anything real yesterday. There's no reason I should be thinking this way about a total stranger, and yet, there's no reason not to.

He's coming back this morning to look at the stairs, and no matter why I'm looking forward to it, I'm going to count my blessings and leave any expectations, worries, even hopes at the door. I'm keeping this simple. That's all my life will allow.

I step slowly and carefully out of the shower and see my phone light up with another text. I am feeling well enough to wrap the towel around my hair today, so I slide into my robe and check the message.

Logan: *I'm leaving my place now. ETA 15 mins. Need me to pick anything up on the way? I'm bringing all the tools I'll need for the job.*

I wipe a trickle of water from my face and message him back.

Me: *No, thanks. I'll make breakfast. But be warned, I'm a terrible cook.*

There's no response as I'm getting dressed and brushing out my wet hair, until finally, as I'm brushing my teeth, I see his response.

Logan: *Breakfast would be great. Believe it or not, no matter how bad, I'm sure I've eaten worse.*

I have a hard time believing he's eaten worse. My

inability to assemble edible food was always a joke between my mother and me. She was a fantastic cook. She could look in the fridge, grab a carrot, leftover chicken, and some spices, and before I knew it, she'd whipped up something that had no name, no "recipe," but somehow tasted delicious.

If I threw the same things in a pan and just let my cooking muse guide me, someone would likely end up with food poisoning, or just plain go hungry. I'm thinking through what I have in the fridge and decide some frozen breakfast sandwiches are the way to go. I don't want to get Logan sick while he's here doing a good deed.

With my hair still wet, I head downstairs, fully dressed and craving some coffee. I look over the check-list they gave me at the hospital and groan.

As I pour my first cup of coffee, Mia wakes up and wanders into the kitchen. She looks super sleepy, but once she sees me moving around, she perks up.

"Am I staying home from school again?" she asks.

Ah shit. I need to call her out again. I didn't manage to do that yesterday, and while I have a couple of missed calls on my phone, I haven't taken the time to check my messages. First call goes to the school. Then I'll deal with work.

I'm just hanging up with the secretary at Mia's

school when there's a knock at the door. Mia barrels down the stairs, Gavin in her hand.

"Mia," I call out. "Let Mama see first."

A smile spreads across my face as I peer through the peephole. When I confirm it's Logan, I nod. "Go ahead," I tell her.

She opens the door, holding Gavin in front of her face. She talks in a funny voice that I assume she means to be Gavin.

"Hi, Logan."

"Gavin." He addresses the toy first, but he looks me in the eye quickly, the hint of a smile on his handsome face. "I've got a question for you, buddy."

He kneels down so he's face-to-face with Gav.

"Do you know what a giraffe's favorite fruit is?"

I can see my daughter grinning as she thinks about the answer. "I don't know. What?" She forgets for a moment to use the Gavin voice, and she's fully beaming at Logan.

"Neck-tarines." Logan waits for her to get the joke, and when she does, her reaction doesn't disappoint.

Mia starts cackling so hard, she drops Gav on the floor. Logan grabs him and, again, brushes off the toy and hands him back to Mia.

"That's a great one," Mia says, then she skips off into the kitchen.

Once we're alone, although not really alone since

Mia's just a few feet away digging in the fridge, Logan grabs a bag of tools and steps inside.

"Good morning." His voice is thick and rich, rolling over my skin like the crashing of a wave against the sand. His dark eyes flash, and he presses his lips together and nods. He looks me over from tip to toe, setting my skin ablaze with warmth.

I shiver and cross my arms over my chest, my still-damp hair feeling very wet and cold against the back of my T-shirt. That's what it is. Not him that is having this effect on me. "Good morning to you," I say. "Great joke."

He steps close to me and admits in a low voice, "I Googled that one. I only had one good giraffe joke, and I used it yesterday."

I smirk. "Your secret's safe with me."

He locks the door and drops his bag of tools by the front door. "How are you?" he asks.

The question feels…personal. Searching and intimate, not a cordial greeting from my friendly neighborhood contractor. But instead of pulling away, I'm drawn in. Closer. It's as if there's a magnetic pull between the two of us that wasn't there yesterday. Or maybe it was, but I was too distracted and sick to notice.

"Logan," I say, feeling a little unsure on my feet. But today, it's not from a headache.

He steps closer and brushes his fingertips, featherlight, against my eyebrow. "That looks good," he says.

"Good?" I chuckle. "You have kind eyes," I say. "I mean, come on. I look like I took a two-by-four to the forehead."

"No." His voice smolders in my ears. "I'm serious. You're healing up good. Wound is clean. Even the bruising isn't as bad as I expected."

"Are you a nurse too?" I ask softly.

He's dressed in work clothes today, a long-sleeved black T-shirt with the sleeves shoved almost to his elbows. I can make out the intricate details of the artwork on his forearms, the light hairs that give his arms a masculine, outdoorsy look. I trace the contours of his body with my eyes—the work jeans that look crisp, almost new. Steel-toe boots, or so I assume, based on the very sturdy-looking design and thick soles.

But it's Logan's face that I can't look away from. Just inches away from me, the crisp scents of citrus and cedarwood left over from soap or maybe aftershave, fill my senses. I'm so grateful I don't have a headache because the fragrance smells good to me, like a long-lost cabin I've been wanting to return to. My lips part as I sweep my eyes over his chin, still scruffy with another day's growth of stubble. The long waves of his black hair are brushed back away from his face. He's staring into my eyes, and it's as if I can see right through to the genuine concern he's feeling. Concern he's feeling for me.

I don't know why he should care, why he should seem so intensely connected to how I'm doing. But his eyes are honest. I can tell that. I feel his emotions pouring off him, and I take a reflexive step back.

"I—I made coffee," I say, turning my back to him. "Come on in."

If he feels the same energy, he hides it, instead ducking his head. He looks uncertain as he glances down at his feet. "My boots... Mind if I leave them on? It'll be safer working with them. I didn't think to bring any shoe covers."

"Of course. It's no problem. Go ahead." I toss a smile back at him, but I scurry into the kitchen, anxious to clear my nose of the mesmerizing scent of his skin. I'm imagining what his stubble would feel like under my fingers. I don't know what the hell's gotten into me. That's a ridiculous, if not dangerous, thought.

I turn on the toaster oven to warm it and pour Logan a cup of coffee. "How do you take it?" I call.

I open the cabinets and pull out plates and flatware, being mindful of how quickly I move. Mia and Logan sit down together at the kitchen table like they've done this a million times before.

Logan listens to Mia chatter about what she wants to do with her day off school while he sips his black coffee. She's telling him about our sleepover on the couch and how she never gets to have sleepovers with her friends anymore, and she misses it.

My attention snags on that little detail, and I look away from the frozen breakfast sandwiches I'm toasting and see Logan, his eyes ever fixed on me.

There's heat there, like he's deep in the same kind of thought I'm battling. But that can't be the case. Whatever this hot man is thinking, it's more likely he's hungry and looking for something to eat than he's thinking about me. I refocus my attention on my girl, who is still sounding a little lost about the lack of friends in her life.

"Baby, you can have a sleepover soon. I promise." I check the breakfast sandwiches and push away a heavy dose of motherly guilt. "I'll call Kylee's mom today," I promise. "Maybe she can sleep over this weekend."

"Yes!" Mia cheers and pushes back from the table. "Can I go play in my room?"

"Honey, you didn't even eat yet." I set a sausage and egg biscuit on the plate in front of Mia. "After breakfast."

Mia's like me and never likes eating breakfast, but if I put the food in front of her, she'll normally dig in. She watches Logan and waits for him to start. "Do you like sausage?" she asks.

He nods. "I'm not too picky when it comes to food," he says, taking a big bite of his sandwich.

"Except pineapple on pizza," I say, remembering what he told me last night.

His eyes meet mine, and a lazy, curious expression curls a smile across his face. "Yeah," he says.

Mia starts moaning about how gross pineapples are, while I stand against the counter and nibble my sandwich.

"Why don't you sit?" Logan says, motioning to a chair.

"I just want to multitask a bit. I need to call my boss. Once you start working, it'll probably be too loud to make any calls."

Logan's face falls. "Is this going to be bad for your head? There's not a lot of pounding involved, but there will be some noise. I never thought maybe it would be a bad day to do this…"

I hold up a hand. "No, no, it'll be fine. I'll just make a few quick calls."

While he dives into his meal, I eat my breakfast and take some over-the-counter pain medicine for my gash. I'm aware of his gaze on me as I punch in my passcode and listen to my voice mail messages. While I was laid up, Mia's school called and my boss.

I call my boss and explain the situation and let him know I'll take a photo of the note from the doctor.

"You realize missing yesterday's meeting put me in a world of hurt." When I get through to him, my boss Jeff is critical. "I'm sorry you were hurt, but I had to cancel the meeting, Bridget. It was your job to prep the quarterly numbers. I can put off the meeting a few days due to your little *situation*, but none of this is good. Not for you, not for me."

I close my eyes and hang my head. "I'm truly sorry for that, Jeff." I try to piece together a sincere apology, but right now, I want to hang up on the guy and climb into bed.

"I didn't want to do this like this, Bridget, over the phone and all, but…"

I squint my eyes closed, but I don't even try to interrupt. I know what's coming. I listen to Jeff say the words that will change my life. They have to let me go. The termination will be for cause.

When he's done, I simply say, "I understand." And then I hang up and drop my face into my hands, my elbows on the kitchen table.

"Hey."

I open my eyes to Logan's concerned expression. He's loaded the dishes into the dishwasher and is standing just a few feet away. Somehow, even at a more than reasonable distance, I feel his heat. Something in me wants to lean in, set my head against that massive shoulder, and just rest. That feeling of safety, of being drawn to someone because there is goodness there, it's not a feeling I'm used to. But I want so badly to trust it.

"I might have earplugs in my tool kit," he says.

"Hmm?" I try to focus and pay attention. Maybe it's the concussion, maybe it's my loneliness—either way, I'm far too focused on the curve of his lips and his strong, uneven nose.

He taps his index finger against his forehead. "I'm worried about making too much noise," he says. "I don't want to do anything to hurt you."

I want to be grateful. I want to talk to him more, reassure him that he's helping me, but I'm hitting a wall hard and fast. I just lost my job, and my stomach is sinking as quickly as my heart. I want to scream, cry, punch something. But I can't do any of that. I need to move slowly and take it easy. My sucky life sucks just a little bit more right now. "It's okay… I just—I…"

"What?" he demands, his tone sharp, almost protective. "What happened?"

I try to play it off lightly, but when the words pass my lips, I start crying. "I got let go. Fired." I shake my head gently and shrug. "Too many days off. Too many sick days for me and Mia. I'd been warned. One more unexcused absence… And yesterday was it."

"Unexcused." His eyes glitter with anger. "Birdie, you were in the hospital. How can they do that?"

"They can," I say quietly. "And they did. It's…it's fine. We'll be okay. I…I'll find something else."

"Come on," he says. "I think you should lie down."

He takes my elbow, and we walk up the stairs together. His hand is firm on me, the other hand hovering but not touching my lower back.

"It's going to be all right," he says. "You've got this."

"I'm not normally helpless, Logan." As much as I need the help, something about being the damsel in distress like this doesn't sit right with me. "I'm not this. I'm more than this," I say, my voice quiet.

At the top of the stairs, he nods at me and says, "I'm going to go look for those earplugs."

Then he heads back downstairs. I go into my bedroom and sit on the edge of the bed. I can hear Mia chattering away, talking to herself.

I hear Logan's boots on the stairs, and suddenly, he's at my bedroom door. He's holding out a small plastic baggie with a bunch of neon orange earplugs inside. "Take a couple," he said. "I'll do my best to work quietly, but you'll want to muffle as much of the noise as you can."

I nod, and he steps inside my bedroom.

"You need water or anything?" he asks as I pick two of the soft foam wedges from the bag.

I laugh. "Logan, I should be asking you that. You're

my guest." I meet his eyes. "Do me a favor? Just make yourself at home. If you need a snack or something to drink, help yourself."

He watches me as I put in the earplugs and lie back against the bed. I have magazines and a book to my right, but I'm so tired, I might just lie here in the dark and rest.

My brain feels like the effort to read or even look at pictures is more than it wants to do. It's as if my mind ran a marathon and my brain is exhausted. I'm not sleepy, but I'm worn-out. It's the strangest feeling.

I'm jobless. Out of options. And I have a shitload of stress ahead. A headache doctor to find. Insurance stuff to sort out.

But for the next few hours, for the first time in a long time, I relax.

8

BRIDGET

WHEN I WAKE UP, MY ROOM IS DARK AND I HEAR nothing. My heart catches in my chest as I remember where I am and what's happened. I'm home in bed. I have a mild concussion after my wild trip down the stairs yesterday.

I shove back the covers and head into the bathroom, noting that Mia's bedroom door is open and I hear not one, but two happy, giggling girls inside.

"Mia?" I tip my head as I peek inside the room. "Who's this?"

My daughter practically launches herself at me as she introduces me to a little girl I don't know.

"Mama," she practically screams. "You're up. You slept so long, right through lunch. This is Zoey, she's my new friend, and…"

Mia's talking loudly and seems so happy, but my

mind is buzzing. Who the hell is this little girl, and what's she doing in my house? I can't decide whether I'm okay with this or angry. Zoey walks up to me and holds out her hand.

"Hi, I'm Zoey," she says. The girl is dressed to the nines in glittery jelly shoes, a sparkly dress, and an adorable hairstyle with lots of colorful bows. She's also wearing nail polish. Mia must be in absolute heaven.

"Hi, Zoey." I shake the girl's hand and debate asking questions, but I think there's someone else whom I should be talking to right now. This child's mother and Logan. "Are you two having fun?" I ask.

Zoey runs up to Mia and gives her a hug. "I love Mia," she says. "I can't believe she's an only child like me. Everyone else at school has brothers or sisters but me. We both love Rainbow Rangers and…"

I hold back a laugh despite my discomfort. This Zoey is a talker, and that is perfect for my Mia. I can see how these two would become instant best friends.

"Mia?" I ask.

"Mama, Zoey is totally my new best friend. We want to have a sleepover this weekend, if it's okay with you and with Zoey's mom. But we already asked Zoey's mom and…"

I hold up my hands. "Okay, kiddo. One step at a time. Why don't you two keep playing while I check on

Logan." What I mean is things downstairs. The work being done. Not the man himself.

Although I wonder for a second if Zoey is Logan's daughter. It seems weird that he wouldn't have mentioned this to me yesterday when he was driving Mia around, but who knows. The whole day was such a mess of confusion and emotion. Either way, there's got to be a reason there's a little girl in my house.

The girls bounce over to Mia's bed and go back to playing without even a goodbye. Mia looks so happy and is having so much fun, some of my instant concern and worry start to melt away. I'm sure there's a reasonable explanation, and it's not like I can get mad when I was sound asleep for what feels like the whole day.

When I reach the top of the stairs, I'm stunned at the amount of work that's been done. I head down the completely clean staircase carefully, out of habit.

Logan is nowhere to be found, but a woman is sitting at my kitchen table, writing some notes in a notepad. She looks up as I approach and leaps from her seat.

"Oh my goodness. You're up. You must be so confused." The woman must be Zoey's mother. They have the same bright eyes and genuine smile. She holds out a hand. "I'm Alice. My daughter Zoey is upstairs with Mia."

"Nice to meet you," I say, my voice unintentionally a little strained. "Where is Logan?"

"Logan?" Alice tips her chin and then bursts out laughing. "You mean Crow. My husband Morris and Crow—Logan—they're in a motorcycle club."

My face must fall a bit when she says motorcycle club because Alice quickly goes on.

"But don't think about what you've seen on TV or in movies," she assures me. "This club isn't into drugs or illegal activities. They don't run guns or do anything shady. They run legitimate businesses, and most of the guys have wives and kids. Like me and Zoey."

She smiles at me, definitely not the stereotypical biker babe. She's slim, even under the loose T-shirt she's wearing, and her shoulder-length hair is piled in a messy bun on top of her head. She's wearing a beautiful sparkly diamond on one hand, and if I didn't know better, I'd guess she was a yoga teacher or something trendy and fun. Seeing how her daughter is dressed and Alice's kind, open face makes me feel at ease immediately.

"Crow wanted to haul your old carpet away," she explains. "Seems like your local trash pickup would have penalized you for throwing construction debris in the regular bins. So, my husband grabbed his truck and came over to help Crow haul the old stuff away. Crow didn't want us to wake you, so I came by to stay with

Mia. I figured since I'm a stranger to her, she might prefer to play with my daughter than have some lady just sitting in her house."

This is all very, very reasonable, but my mind is blown. Who are these people who just show up for one another like it's no big deal? Alice had nothing better to do on a weekday than bring her husband and kid to a stranger's house?

Not only that, but Crow…

The tattoos and his tough-as-nails exterior make a little more sense now. I'm not sure what to think about the fact that he left my daughter alone with a strange woman, but since I was home and asleep… God, this is weird.

"You must be starving." Alice waves me over to the fridge. "I brought Crow lunch when I came by. Plenty of extras. Can I offer you something?"

The room starts to spin. This woman is in my house, offering me food. The fragile grip I have on my circumstances makes me feel vulnerable enough. But when it's just Mia and me, I don't have to explain or apologize to anyone. Having people in and out of my house like this, in and out of my business… I feel so exposed. And I hate how lacking this makes me feel.

"No, no… I'm okay." I shake my head and squint against a slight spark of pain.

Alice gathers her papers from the table and smiles.

"Now that you're up, why don't I take Zoey and head home? Give you back your space."

She's so nice and seems so thoughtful, I feel like an asshole for wanting this woman to leave. But it's a lot to absorb in just a few minutes. I'm about ready to ask her to leave when the front door opens.

Two enormous men are talking in hushed voices. Logan comes through the door first, a huge, relaxed grin on his face. Seeing him like that, looking light and happy, strikes me. He's so serious, so focused, that something loosens in my chest at the family feeling he seems to have with the other guy. Morris, I assume.

"The lady of the house." The second man is wearing a baby-blue T-shirt that stretches comically over his giant biceps. He's got a bandanna around his head, and he tugs it off with one hand and mops sweat from his brow. In spite of his size and gruff look, he's got a huge smile and he holds out a hand to me, but then pulls it back. "I'd shake your hand, ma'am," he says, "but I worked up quite the sweat out there. Pleased to meet you. Name's Morris."

I look from him to Alice, who is watching him and just beaming. "Honey," she says, "I think all these people in Bridget's house is a bit much. We should leave her to rest. I was just going to get Zoey."

He nods and gives Logan a slap on the shoulder. "Catch up to ya later, brother. You did good work here."

Logan nods, accepting the praise. "Thanks for the hand, man. Couldn't have done it without your truck."

Morris calls up the stairs, "Zoey. We got to go."

I must have winced at the sound, because Logan tenses and Morris shakes his head.

"Oh shit. I'm an ass. Apologies. I didn't think."

I wave a hand. "It's okay. I'm okay. I should thank you for what you did here. I'm sorry I'm... I'm not at my best today."

That is true. With the darkness of my deep sleep fading away and the shock of finding strangers in the house with my daughter, I realize my defenses are sky-high.

There is nothing more to this than a contractor calling on a friend to help him haul away my trash. And they were kind enough to bring along someone to make sure my daughter wasn't essentially home alone with a passed-out mother.

Clearly, Mia is having no problem accepting these people, because neither she nor Zoey seem to listen to Morris's call.

Alice is at my side, her bag full of papers in her hands. "I think we may have to break up the new best friends in a slightly more direct way." She grins at me. "Mind if I go up and get my daughter?"

"Of course."

While Alice heads up the stairs, Morris and Logan talk quietly about supply costs, materials, and permits.

"Only the GC would need a license, so we'll have Alice look through the specs and build a budget." Morris is explaining things to Logan, and he's nodding, but his eyes never leave my face.

Zoey comes down the stairs hand in hand with Mia.

"Mama." Mia runs up to me and claps her arms around my waist. "Can Zoey come back for a sleepover this weekend? Please."

Alice shakes her head and says, "Mia, your mama might need a little more time to recover before I let my wild angel loose on your house for a whole sleepover. But I'll make sure Bridget has my number in case she wants to set up another playdate."

Alice looks at me and asks, "Is it okay if I get your number from Crow?"

I nod, watching Mia and Zoey hug like they never want to say goodbye. But they do, and Zoey literally jumps from Mia's arms to Morris's in one leap.

"Off we go, Zoey," he says. He waves to me. "Nice meeting you, Bridget." Then he maneuvers around so Zoey can ride on his back, and he heads off toward a huge pickup truck parked in front of the house.

Alice touches Logan's cheek as she passes by. "Come for dinner?" she asks.

He nods. "Yeah, soon. Thanks, Alice."

Alice waves and smiles, and then it's just me and Logan and my girl.

"Mama." Mia is wound up, hyper and in a great mood. "Zoey did the funniest thing. I have to tell you everything."

"I want you to, sweetie," I say, bending over to hug her. "But can I have a minute to catch up with Logan?"

She runs up my newly bare stairs and goes back to playing in her room. "Come up when you're done, and I'll show you what we made."

I sigh in spite of myself. I'm happy that Mia made a friend. I'm grateful Logan had help with the stairs. But this is all becoming much more complicated than I ever expected. Help with a bit of loose carpet is one thing, but all this...

"I ran into a small snag," Logan says, his voice low. "Some of the steps need to be replaced. Now that the carpet and the padding are gone, you can hear the rot when you step." He walks up to the staircase and puts his full weight on one of the stairs. The wood squeaks, and I can see a little bit of give when he shifts back and forth. "It's safe for now for you and Mia to walk up and down, but I'd like to come back and replace a bit of the wood. That's a bigger job, though. More mess, more noise."

He's looking at me as though asking my permission,

but the truth is, I feel as if I've lost control of my own life.

"Right." I turn away and head into the kitchen. I'm hungry and confused. This doesn't feel like me. Hours ago, I was thinking about Logan's muscular arms and sexy chin, and now I'm not sure what I've gotten myself into. I feel crabby, groggy, and out of control.

"Hey, Bridget, did I do something?" Logan follows me into the kitchen. "Did you eat? Alice brought sandwiches—"

"I'm not hungry." My words are sharp, the edges intended to cut.

From the look on Logan's face, I did, in fact, hurt him. The lightness in his face from when his friends were here fades, and that shadowy mask comes back up.

"I get it." He pulls out his phone and punches in a text. "I'll gather my stuff. You look like you're ready to have your house back."

Part of me doesn't want him to rush out. I just want all the confusing and frustrating feelings to slow down. I feel like I need more time to process, to think through what's going on. It's as if I can tell the wheels in my brain are spinning much more slowly, fighting their way through a light fog. I'm not disoriented, but I'm also just feeling irritable about everything. As good as it felt to rest, now things are happening, and I don't have any control of my own house, my life.

I'm trying to decide whether I should apologize or be apologized to, or neither, when I hear the faint honk of a horn outside. Logan meets me in the kitchen where I'm still standing, staring into the sink.

"Bridget?" His voice is soft. Understanding, but also still hurt.

"Crow, wait," I say. "I-I'm sorry. I don't mean to seem ungrateful. Thank you for all you did today. The stairs look great, and I... I can't believe your friends just showed up like that to help. I'm a little overwhelmed."

"Believe me, I get that. You need rest and quiet, not a stream of people running through your place." He nods, and he sounds a lot less hurt. "I'm incredibly fortunate to have the brotherhood I do," he says cryptically. "They are more than I deserve. And these days, the guys come with wives and kids that somehow sort of complete the package."

He looks happy again, like he did when Morris and Alice were here. The dark intensity of his eyes is warmer now, and I can see his beautiful lips part in a full smile.

"Here are your keys," he says. "I texted Morris to come back and give me a ride." He sets my key chain on the counter and steps a little closer. "Don't drive yet," he says. "Okay? Follow the doctor's orders as best you can. If you need anything, you know how to reach me. When you're feeling better, if you want to talk about the rest of the work on the stairs, the invitation's wide open."

I feel him hesitate at my side, but when I turn, he's walked to the bottom of the stairs and is calling for Mia. But he surprises me by addressing my daughter's stuffed animal.

"I got to roll, Gavin. Take good care of Miss Mia." His voice isn't loud, but it's loud enough for Mia to hear him.

She runs to the top of the stairs. "Are you coming back tomorrow?" she asks. "Are you going to finish the stairs?"

Logan just smiles. "I'll wait until your mom's ready for more noise and mess in her house." He gives her a nod and then looks at me. "Birdie."

He says my name, and Mia runs back to her room, calling out for me to come see what she made with Zoey. Bag in hand, he heads toward the front door but stops before he leaves. He turns to me, and those intense eyes meet mine.

"You said something earlier," he says, his eyes never leaving mine. "That you're not this. That you're more than this." He presses his lips together. "You're not the only one who feels that way about their life. Sometimes, the sum of the parts doesn't look like much more than a pile of shit. But that doesn't mean the parts are bad. You might just need to reassemble. That's what

I'm trying to do." He looks down at his feet and then yanks open the door. "You know how to reach me," he says.

And then he's gone.

I lock the door behind him and wander into the kitchen. His friend Alice has left a small assortment of sandwiches and a large salad in my fridge. My stomach gurgles at the food, but first, I want to check on my baby.

I don't know why I'm so irritable, so sensitive. Maybe it's the stress of the last twenty-four hours. But something about my feelings doesn't feel *right*. Under normal circumstances, I would have been the first person to invite these people in. To make small talk and enjoy the company. I miss the days when Mom would have friends over after work, older ladies, mostly widows or divorcées. Mom never dated after Dad, but she had a crocheting circle, volunteer groups... She wouldn't have shut down strangers in her house for any reason.

I miss her presence more than ever. I walk up the smooth stairs, marveling at how quickly he removed the carpeting. And I slept through the whole thing. When I make it upstairs, I tap on Mia's door and plop down beside her on the bed.

"What a day, huh, kiddo? Want to tell me everything?"

Mia is drawing something incredibly complex, and I lean over to look.

"Is this what you did with...what was her name?" I can't believe I can't remember the little girl's name... Shit. "Zoey."

Memory loss, mood changes. It's hard to deny that I'm dealing with a mild concussion. No matter how badly I want to be totally fine and normal, I'm not.

"Yes. Look, Mama." Laid out on Mia's bed are a dozen sheets of paper with pencil drawings made by two different hands. I can make out the distinctive drawings that Mia made, the eyes of all the characters big and round, and I assume the other elements were made by Zoey.

I'm trying to make out what all the characters are doing, but Mia walks me through each frame.

"We wrote a story." She traces the animals and figures that Zoey drew, reverently explaining that Zoey is older and has a better grasp on animal anatomy than Mia does. They drew page after page—together on the same sheet of paper. Artwork illustrating an adventure between a little girl who doesn't have a best friend and who is on the hunt to find one. She tries riding an elephant and playing with dolphins, but the girl's story isn't finished. The kids ran out of time.

"So, does the little girl find her best friend?" I ask,

stroking my daughter's hair. I feel I already know the answer, but I want to hear it from her.

"I hope so, but Zoey and I have a lot more to draw before the end. Can she come back this weekend, Mama? Please," she begs, more intently this time.

Whoever these people are, whatever I did to bring them into my life, I close my eyes and nod.

It may be hard for me to accept help, to welcome new people into the mess that is my life, but Mia is that little girl without a best friend. And Zoey probably is too in some ways. If life brought someone to us who can fill that role, there's no chance I'm going to stand in their way.

I pick up my phone and compose a text to Logan, making plans for the weekend.

9

CROW

When Saturday rolls around, I'm up before sunrise. I'm in the kitchen of the compound, making some coffee and trying not to get ahead of myself.

Today, I'm starting the repair to Birdie's stairs.

We've been texting every day since I pulled the carpeting off her stairs. Nothing big. Me checking in on her. Talking about my day. Getting caught up on how she's been feeling. She sent Mia back to school with some carpooling help from the other moms and has set up all her doctor appointments for the coming weeks. She's been resting, and even though it's only been a few days, she's feeling well enough to think about trying to find a job.

I think it's too soon. The ER doc said a week to ten days, so when I see her today, my plan is to let her know how I feel. She only gets one chance to heal from a concussion, and rushing it…

At the same time, I know what being unemployed means. She's got a house that, I don't know, probably has a mortgage and a kid who needs feeding.

My phone buzzes with a new voice mail. I'm checking my phone when Morris rolls into the compound.

"Yo, yo," he says, clapping me on the shoulder. "You ready to roll?"

"You're early, man." I check the time on my phone and nod. The call was from a New York number. One I don't recognize, so it's not Birdie, and it's not something I want to deal with today.

"Tell me about it." Morris rubs his eyes and yawns loudly. "Zoey was up at the butt-crack of dawn, begging me to take her to Mia's. *It's Saturday, Dad. It's Saturday. Can we leave?* To have the energy of a kid." He's groaning, but I've known Morris long enough to know he's loving every minute of it.

"Dad?" I repeat.

"Yeah, yeah." He chuckles. "That never gets old. I love the sound of it every time." He lifts his chin at me. "You thinking about kids?"

"What?" I dump the last bit of coffee into the sink and load my mug into the dishwasher. I toss him a look. "Where the hell's that coming from?"

He crosses his arms over his T-shirt. He's wearing his leather vest over it, so he looks more like the old Morris than the dad version of the brother I remember from before. That man wore leather, cursed up a storm, and could drink three times his body weight in beer. Now, I feel like I've got a grizzled, tattooed dad trying to give me life lessons.

"Bridget's single, right?"

I slip my phone into my pocket and pull my sunglasses over my eyes. "Doesn't matter if she is or isn't."

"Why not? She's hot, unattached, as far as you know. Great kid."

I know Morris is trying to make a point, but it's having the opposite effect. "You just listed every reason she's not going to want anything to do with me." I look at Morris and, for the first time, admit what's burning under the surface. "Come on, man. A guy with a record? I killed a guy. You think she's going to want me around her kid when she finds that out? I'm just going to do the work and hopefully end up with a reference when it's all done. Nothing more."

Morris shrugs. "Suit yourself. You're not the only one who's running from the past. A lot of people do. Maybe not from a record, but I can't look at a single person I know who doesn't think their shit stinks worse than everybody else's. Maybe to her, your shit's not all that bad."

"It's early for the deep fucking thoughts, Morris." I clap my brother on the back. "But I get it."

It doesn't change anything, though. If I'd met Bridget seven years ago... Shit. Right about the time I was getting my ass locked up, she was giving birth to Mia. She's raised a kid on her own, lost her mother... Somehow, next to that, my life seems too dark and totally out of place. I don't see how there's room in her life for a guy like me.

Which is why I have to shove aside the way she makes me feel. Pretend that I'm not more excited about seeing her than I am about doing a job that could lead to more work. I'm just going to go in, no expectations. Except the expectation that I'm putting on myself now. That I do my job and do it well. That way, I probably won't be disappointed.

Morris drops me off in front of Bridget's house just as Alice and Zoey are pulling up. Morris hands me the keys to his truck and meets his wife on the sidewalk. Zoey's carrying a backpack so loaded with who knows what that she can hardly carry it, so Morris slings the backpack over one shoulder and grabs Zoey's hand. They walk up to the front door, while Alice greets me.

"Are you coming to Lia's baby shower next week-end?" she asks. "You're welcome to invite Bridget. It'll be kid-friendly, and I think Zoey would love having Mia there."

I shake my head, but I don't know what to say. Alice and Morris are clearly playing matchmaker, but they've got it all wrong. I give Alice a look, but then I just decide to say what's on my mind.

"Would you date a man like me?" I point to Zoey, who's jumping up and down with excitement on the front stoop while they wait for Bridget to open the door. "Little kid, single mom, and a convict?"

"Ex-convict," she corrects me. "Crow," she says gently. "Some of the best people I know have the worst luck. And some of the worst people look like heroes on paper."

I'm sure Alice is talking about her ex. The dude was manipulative and borderline abusive. I don't think he laid a hand on her, but he had a choke hold on her soul, from what Morris says. The fact that the guy tried to burn down the building where Alice worked after he found out she'd left him tells me everything I need to know about the piece of shit. Prison is the right place for a son of a bitch like that.

When it comes to me, though, I'm sure Alice is biased. She's only known me a month, and everything she's heard has been filtered through Morris.

Alice is still looking at me with such kindness, I want to squirm. "Thanks," I mumble, not because I really believe her, but because it's the right thing to say.

Then I head up to the house, where Birdie has opened the door for Morris and Zoey.

It's adorable to see how excited the girls are to see each other. Even though Zoey and Mia have only known each other for a few days, they are hugging, squealing, and they start taking everything out of Zoey's backpack just inside the front door. I stop right in the doorway and am looking down at enough colored pencils and crayons to fill an entire preschool when Bridget greets me.

She reaches out her hand. "This house was full of trip hazards before. Now…"

I take her hand and step over the backpack. "Whoa," I say.

She's looking at me as I release her hand. "Good morning. Crow." She says my nickname like she's trying it on.

"Good morning, Birdie." I don't mean for that to come out the way it does. It's optimistic. Flirtatious, maybe. I'm so out of practice, I don't even know what my intention here is. Bridget smiles, but Alice's grin is even bigger. They start talking about logistics for the girls, and I hear Mia begging her mom to let Zoey have a sleepover.

Morris clears his throat loudly. "Ladies, I got a hot date waiting for me."

Alice rolls her eyes. "He's going for a ride with Tiny today, but not until I drop him back at the compound." She looks at Zoey. "I'll pick you up around three, okay? Listen to Bridget, and remember to mind your manners."

I'm glad to hear Alice is planning to come back later to get Zoey. As much as the kids want to hang out, I don't know if a sleepover is the best thing for Bridget right now. She's not even a week out from her fall, and with all the noise I'm going to be making today, she's going to need quiet tonight to rest.

While Morris and Alice say their goodbyes to Zoey, I make a quick list of the supplies I'll need from the hardware store. I won't need much, but I don't want to use scrap lumber to fix the stairs. I let Bridget know I'm heading out too and will be back with supplies in just a bit.

She hands me two twenty-dollar bills. "Will this cover the supplies?" she asks. Her gray eyes are stormy, the welcoming, almost flirtatious Bridget of a few minutes ago gone.

I wave off her money.

"I got this, Birdie. And don't argue."

She shakes her head, a reluctant smile on her pretty face. "Well, thank you. I appreciate that."

I follow Morris out, wish him and Alice goodbye, then run to the hardware store to get what I'll need for the day, plus a fresh pair of earplugs for Bridget. When I get back, the kids are at the kitchen table having a snack. Bridget's sipping something from a mug.

"Coffee?" I ask, setting the lumber I need on a drop cloth.

She shoos the girls upstairs to play. "Yeah, want some?" she asks.

"I was thinking about your head. You're all good with the caffeine now?"

She pours me a cup and nods. "I am, but I'm taking it easy. Just a half cup, plenty of milk." She pours me a cup. "Do you only have a motorcycle?" she asks.

"Only a motorcycle?" I echo, not sure what she's getting at.

"You always get rides from your friends. I wasn't sure if you own a car or if it's because you bring tools and stuff here that you can't carry on a motorcycle."

"Yeah. Only my bike for now." I look into her rain-cloud eyes and search for what she's really after. Is she interested in me or just making conversation with the man who's going to be in her house all day? If you can still call me a stranger after I've watched her kid, driven her around.

The room lights up when she's in it, and I feel myself both speed up and slow down when she's around. My heart, my body—everything seems to fall into place around her, and yet... It shouldn't. Back in the day, I would have bought her a drink, taken her to bed, and put any feelings in my rearview, but now... Now, I don't even know how to talk to this woman because I'm damned sure, no matter what I feel, no matter what seems real, there are some walls that are too high to climb.

She sips her coffee, and the smile she gives me makes me want to open up. Makes me want to share myself with her—what I've been through. What I'm feeling. But I know too well that telling her anything—forget about telling her everything—might get me kicked out of this house.

"I've been through a rough patch. My friends have rallied around me, though." Shame and uncertainty make me duck my head as I grunt, "I'm going to get started." I drop the earplugs on the kitchen table. "I'll do my best to keep the noise down."

She looks surprised, like she was expecting to talk more, but she nods and takes the earplugs. I start prepping the tools for the job, and she walks up to me, the earplugs in one hand and her coffee mug in the other.

"Mind if I go upstairs?"

I move aside to let her pass. When she reaches halfway up the stairs, she stops and looks back at me. "You must be incredibly special to have friends who rally around you like that," she says. "Good people tend to stick together. And your friends seem like good people."

I don't respond. Don't know what to say. I'm not sure if she's thinking about her own situation and the lack of friends rallying around her right now, or if she really means to pay me a compliment.

I grunt again and get to work, but the longer I let her words sink in, the more they mean to me. She's right. Morris and I go way back.

Although, the more time passes, the more I realize the true things in my life haven't changed all that much. Not Morris. Not my place in the MC. Not how they treat me. It's as if not even a day has passed. And that same vibe extends to me from Alice. She has no reason to be kind to me. No reason to nudge me into asking Bridget out. They are good people. Good friends. But I suspect the way they treat me is more about them than it is about me.

I shove aside all the thinking and feeling and get to work. I'm halfway through repairing the stairs when I realize I have enough time and cash to make a handrail for the wall. I'll need the right length of wood, though, which means heading back to the store. I stalk up the stairs and knock lightly on Bridget's open bedroom door.

I can hear the girls in Mia's room, laughing and talking. It makes me smile. They sound so happy and free. I can't remember that feeling anymore, what it feels like to have no weight on my shoulders, no pressure on my chest. It's as if I've been carrying my pain so long, I wouldn't know how to put it down if I could.

"Hey," I call out.

Bridget's lying on her bed, her phone in hand. She's got the earplugs in, which means she doesn't hear me. I step into her room, waving my hand in front of me so I don't scare the shit out of her.

"Oh. Crow."

Hearing that word on her lips does something to me. It feels foreign and old, but so, so good. As if she's connecting to a part of me that I didn't think she'd ever see. She pulls out the earplugs and pats the edge of her bed. "How's it going?"

I washed my hands downstairs, but I might have sawdust on my pants and shirt, so I don't want to sit. But she's watching me, waiting, so I carefully ease down on the corner of the bed.

"S'going good," I say. "Not the comedy show that's going on in there." I motion toward Mia's room. "But good. I have enough time to put up a handrail on that wall if you'd like. I need to hit the hardware store for the right length of wood and the brackets, but if you're okay with it, I can put that up today too."

She looks surprised but nods. "That'd be great, if you have the time."

I nod and start to get up, but she stops me.

"I've been texting your friend Alice. She's invited me and Mia to a baby shower next weekend. One of your motorcycle buddies."

I chuckle at that, and she flushes, a generous pink that creeps from her pretty throat to her cheeks.

"Is that the wrong word?"

"Nah, you're fine," I say.

"Well, Alice said Mia can sleep over with Zoey after the baby shower. Lia and Leo are having a baby, and Alice and Morris are hosting the party, so she said it would be great to have someone Zoey can play with. She seems excited that the girls are getting along."

I nod. "Yeah. I'm sure it'll be a great time."

"Will you be there?" she asks almost shyly.

The question throws me, and I scrub a hand over my chin. "I mean… I hadn't decided, to be honest. But I could go. It's usually a chick thing."

"Well, no, I mean…not if you weren't planning on it. I just thought maybe we could go together. Or, if you're going to be there, I'd at least see you. You know, under better circumstances. When you're not working and when I'm not hospitalized." Her lips twist into a sweet, sly smile.

"You want to do that?" I ask. "Hang out?"

"Mmm-hmm." She smiles. "I'd like that."

As much as I should want this, as much as I should

be over the fucking moon that a gorgeous woman like her would want to spend time with me, the whole thing is just too complicated.

I don't say anything for a second, just staring at her like a dumbfuck, when she looks away. "Crow, I...I Googled you."

My mouth immediately goes dry, and something in my stomach tightens as if I've been punched in the gut.

She moves, kicking her legs over the side of the bed so we're sitting side by side. "I know that might seem invasive, like I violated your privacy, but..."

"What does that mean?" I demand.

Everything she says after that is a blur. I can't hear her through the buzzing in my head. I might not have known what Googling someone meant six months ago, but now, I know exactly what she's getting at. I've Googled myself plenty of times to see what prospective employers might find when they run background checks on me.

There are only two very small write-ups about what happened at the bar that night. One in the local county paper's police blotter and a slightly bigger write-up after the trial. But my name, my picture, and the whole goddamn story is out there. And she found it.

"It's okay," she says, putting a hand on my shoulder. "I read the—"

I can't listen to this. My mind is spinning, and the

coffee I drank earlier turns sour in my stomach. I get up from the bed and nod at her. "Right. Yeah. I need to go."

I head down the stairs, but Bridget follows after me. "Crow?" she calls, but I keep walking. "Logan, please, can we just talk?"

I look over the tools and materials, all the shit I need to clean up before I can leave. But Bridget's right behind me, coming down the stairs, her gray eyes dark and her hair loose and flowing over her shoulders. "Logan, please?"

I turn to face her. I want to stay. I want to talk to her. I want to open up to someone, but I'm not sure I know how to do that anymore. I'm not even sure I know who I am anymore. I'm trapped between the old me and the way I would have behaved and the new me. The man who has to anticipate people's reactions to him. The old Crow didn't give a fuck. And that was the attitude that got me into this mess. I threw a punch and put some cocksucking meth head in his place, and in the blink of an eye, my future was gone. Dead and buried, right in front of my eyes.

My phone buzzes in my pocket, so I pull it out, Birdie watching my every move with a sincere, pained look on her face. I swipe to read the text from Madge.

Hey sexy, your brother called. Just fyi. I gave him your number so he'd know how to reach you.

Fuckin' Madge.

She gave this number to my brother, which means my father will have it too. I was pretty sure that New York number from this morning had to be my dad, but I still haven't listened to the voice mail. I'm not ready for the calls to start. The questions.

I jam the phone into my pocket and head for the door. "I'm sorry," I say. "I have to run."

Before Bridget has a chance to say another word, I'm in Morris's truck, driving away.

10

BRIDGET

I'm a complete and total asshole. I realize that as I watch Crow drive away in Morris's truck. I close the front door and sink down on the couch.

Why the hell did I tell him I'd Googled him?

I suppose, on some level, I thought it would make things easier for him. I know about his past, and I don't judge him. In fact, quite the opposite. It never occurred to me that he'd be upset that I knew or that I didn't give him a chance to tell me if he was ever going to, in his way, in his time. I wish I could chalk it up to my recent injuries, but honestly, I'm just so out of practice with matters of the heart. Although I don't know if it's my heart that's reacting every time I think of Logan—or something else.

This thing I feel around him, whether it's chemistry

or interest or whatever it is… I thought if he was feeling anything like what I am…

Fuck.

I don't know what I was thinking. He knows my shit —he's had a front-row seat for it. My money problems and broken-down house. I figured I'd save us some unnecessary drama if he knew that I'd read about his incarceration and that I am okay with it.

But that was clearly a misstep on my part.

I grab my phone and think about texting him. I mean, he has to come back, right? He didn't grab his tools or his materials. Alice is coming later to get Zoey, so I suppose she could pack everything up and take it to him. He might be gone for good.

The reality that I might never see him again makes something tighten in my chest. I shouldn't have any feelings about this, about this man, but they're there or, at least, something is. Disappointment. Uncertainty. Regret. All the things I feel just about every day, but now I have something to focus them on. Just a few days of knowing Crow, and I felt like I was getting *to know him*. The late-night texts all week sure as hell felt like the prelude to something.

The man who makes giraffe jokes with my kid. The man who showed up to fix my stairs without the promise of anything but a kind word about his work.

The man whose corded arms and bearded jaw make me feel alive, awake for the first time in forever.

A lot of things about Logan make sense now that I know his story. But it's not enough for me to piece it all together on my own. I want to hear it from him. I want to listen, understand, and give him the support I'll bet he's used to only getting from people like Morris and Alice. People who loved the man he was and stood by him. Who know the man he is now, no matter how long he was away.

I can hear Mia and Zoey upstairs laughing, and I wonder for a minute if I've completely misjudged the situation.

God, I'm an ass.

I'm a broke single mom with a headache condition. Maybe he isn't interested in *me*. Maybe the reason he hauled ass out of here is because he doesn't want to be saddled with someone else and their problems when he's got more than enough on his own plate.

And I just violated his privacy but digging into his past and throwing it in his face. No wonder he stormed out of here. I wouldn't blame him if he left his tools and blocked my number.

Feeling miserable, I look out the peephole and hope against hope that I see him walking up the walkway, but there's nothing. My car's on the street where Crow parked it last. His tools, materials, drop cloth, and everything are still spread out in my foyer.

I walk up the stairs, admiring his work as I go. The stairs are clean and the workspace dust-free. He must have finished the stairs and was going to add on the handrail. Gone are the spongy parts and the squeaks. My stairs are like new. Safe and strong. Just like I wish I could be.

I'm at the top of the stairs when there's a knock at the door. I head back down, my heart throbbing in my chest. He's back... Maybe he'll let me explain...

But when I open the door, it's Alice.

"Hi." She's so cheerful and sunny. "How was your day?"

I'm stunned to see her standing there. "I'm surprised to see you," I say, blurting out the truth.

"Oh no, really? It's three o'clock. The time must have really flown by." She's standing on the stoop, and I open the door and motion her in.

"I can't believe it's three. Come in, please." She follows me inside and eyes the stairs.

"That looks fantastic. Did he get it all done?" She's looking around and noticing Logan's not here. She cocks her head. "Is Crow here? Did he leave? Morris's truck is parked out front, I just assumed he'd still be here."

The truck is out front? I look through the front

curtains, and sure enough, parked on the opposite side of the street is the distinctive pickup that belongs to Alice's husband.

I look at Alice, this woman I hardly know, and sink down onto my couch. I rest my face in my hands. "I screwed up, big-time."

"I know a thing or two about screwing up. It used to be my specialty." Alice sits beside me. "Want to share?"

"The kids," I start. "Do you want to check on Zoey?"

Alice grins. "I can hear they're doing just fine. I've got time."

I start to tell her that I Googled Logan, but she interrupts me with a hand on my arm.

"Are you into him? Like into him, into him?" She's grinning so big I'm sure that my being attracted to him can't be a bad thing. I mean, I don't even know if he has a wife or girlfriend... That wasn't information I was able to find by cybersnooping.

"It's been so long since I dated anyone, and I just..." I rub my face with my hands and wince at the slight sting of pain over my still-healing eyebrow.

"He's hot," Alice fills in. "I mean, come on. Any woman with eyes can see that."

I chuckle, feeling better since she's the one who said it. "God, isn't he, though? I mean, he's got the tall, dark, and handsome thing, but then he's also so serious and yet playful at the same time."

Alice nodded. "I know. I've got one of those myself. Morris looks like he'd tear the face off anyone who looked at me funny, but then two minutes later, he's braiding Zoey's hair."

I sigh deeply, relieved that she gets it.

"So, what did you find?" she presses. "When you Googled him. You found some news articles, I'm guessing?"

I nod. "Yeah. And I feel really, really bad. I know he went to prison. I tried to explain that it doesn't matter, but…"

Just then, there's another knock at the door. This one firm. Loud.

Alice looks at me, and I get up to cheek the peep-hole. I open the door, and Logan greets us both.

"Alice," he says with a nod. Then softer, "Birdie."

He's holding a piece of unfinished wood in his hands, the perfect length and shape for a handrail.

"Am I interrupting? I was going to get back to work," he says, then kneels back down in front of his tools and materials.

"Not interrupting at all. I'm going to pry my daughter away from Birdie's," Alice says. "I have a feeling the begging is about to begin. Zoey is desperate for a sister, but I have a feeling..." She pats her stomach.

"Wait, what?" I stand and walk over to her. "Alice, are you...?"

Logan's head whips up, and we look at each other for a moment before we look at her.

"Shh," she whispers. "Morris and I have only told Zoey so far. We don't want to take any of the excitement of Lia and Leo's baby shower away from them. We'll tell everyone after that's over. But Zoey is so excited, all she can do is pick out names and plan games. She's going to be a great big sister, but I have a feeling she's going to be very disappointed when this little nugget turns out to be a brother. We had to bribe her that she can name her sibling if she keeps this secret until after the shower. It'll be a miracle if we don't end up with a kid named after a Rainbow Ranger."

I start to laugh, because that takes real faith. If I let Mia name another human being, I can almost guarantee it wouldn't turn out well. My mom helped her name Gavin the giraffe after Mia wanted to name him "Giraffey."

Crow is beaming. "Morris...a dad. A mini-Morris." He stands up from his work and walks over to Alice. "Congratulations."

She wraps her arms around him and laughs, lifting up on her toes and squeezing him tight. "We're thrilled.

It wasn't expected, but it's a very happy accident. Although it's a secret for now. Got it?"

"Got it. Lips are sealed, babe."

When Alice releases Logan, even though I hardly know her, I'm grinning and pulling her in for a hug. "Congratulations. How far along are you?"

"It's early," she says. "Not even ten weeks, so we've got a long way to go, but I'm feeling surprisingly good. Just tired. That's part of the reason I'm so happy that Zoey has found someone she can have fun with. It's going to be hard after being an only child all this time to have a baby to compete with. And I just haven't had the same energy I normally do to run around and keep her entertained." Alice releases me from the hug and meets my eyes. "I'm so glad you've come into our lives. I think our girls are going to need each other."

She walks up the stairs, calling for Zoey. I can already hear the groans of annoyance and Zoey begging her mom for more time.

When we're alone downstairs, I study Logan's face. I hope like hell he's going to let me apologize, but he looks happy and light.

"A baby. God, that's good news." He looks down at his hands. "You know, not that long ago, one of us knocking somebody up wouldn't have been something to celebrate." He looks at me. "But times change. People change."

He bends down to get back to work, and I open my mouth to say something, to walk through the door I feel he's opened just a crack, but Alice is already heading back down the stairs, both of our daughters putting up quite a fight about separating.

"Mama, can Zoey spend the night? Please."

I laugh at Mia's theatrics, but Zoey's got her beat.

"Mom," Zoey deadpans, "you wouldn't believe how fast the time flew. We hardly had enough time to get started. We had to break for lunch, and with all the setup…seriously. We need more time. Can I please, please stay? I promise not to stay up all night."

Alice is firm. "Absolutely not. Don't forget, Bridget is still recovering. She doesn't need to be responsible for two wildlings." Alice puts her hands on Zoey's shoulders. "And you know you are incapable of going to sleep early when you have a sleepover. I'm sorry, but I can't let you inconvenience Bridget like that tonight. Maybe when she's all better, if Bridget thinks it's okay."

"Why don't we bring Mia to our house instead? We won't keep anyone up there, and we can stay up all night."

Alice bends to meet her daughter's face and holds her cheeks between her palms. "You realize that's really not selling me on the idea, right?"

But Mia jumps on that and wraps her arms around

my waist. "That's such a good idea, Mama. Can I? Can I sleep over at Zoey's?"

I look at Alice, tilting my chin. "Honey, Alice didn't plan on an overnight guest tonight. I don't know if…" I look at the woman. I hardly know her, but I have met her husband. They invited me to a baby shower next week. I don't know these people, but is it really all that different from the kids Mia knows from school having a sleepover? It's not like I go over and do a house inspection every time my daughter has a playdate. While I do insist on meeting both parents before letting her have sleepovers with anybody, that's a box I can already check with Alice and Morris.

"I'm fine with it if you are," Alice says. "Morris is going to be out riding with Tiny until probably suppertime, so having Mia around will keep Zoey entertained." Alice looks at me. "We were thinking of picking up Chinese food for dinner. Is that okay with Mia?"

"I love Chinese." Mia seems so happy. Nothing like the responsible, worn-out little girl she's had to be the last few months. After what she's been through this week, I feel like she deserves to have some fun with her new friend.

"Are you sure it's no trouble?" I ask. "Really, Alice, if you think—"

Alice shakes her head. "Honestly, you'll be doing me a favor. I've been more tired than usual, if you know what I mean, so having someone keep up with Zoey will be great. Morris and I can catch up on our shows tonight, guilt-free."

I look at Alice and Zoey, then to Mia. This is all so unexpected, happening so fast. But I guess that's how life happens. And this is a good thing for my daughter, so I don't hesitate to accept the offer.

"Pack your toothbrush," I remind Mia. "And no staying up all night. When Alice says it's time to quiet down and get some sleep—"

The girls are squealing and hugging again, and I can't help but feel happy for them. They thunder up the stairs, and I can hear Zoey telling Mia that maybe now her mom will let her get bunk beds.

"You're going be sleeping over all the time, and we can't just rough it in sleeping bags."

Alice is laughing and shaking her head. "Rough it," she echoes.

She makes sure I have every possible phone number I could need—her cell phone, Morris's, the office number, and even the compound number. "Just in case," she says. She also gives me her home address and asks if I know the neighborhood.

"I do," I say.

"Well, you come by any time tomorrow, and... Oh, nope, nope. Never mind. You shouldn't drive yet, right? I'll run Mia back tomorrow in the afternoon. I'll call first to see if you need anything before I come by."

"No, really, that's okay. I can do it. You're doing enough just keeping her for the night."

Logan is giving me a look but doesn't say anything.

"Well, we can figure that out tomorrow," Alice says.

We compare notes on food allergies and house rules for a minute, but then the kids come back down the stairs, and I swear I've never seen my child look happier.

"I'll give you my car seat," I say and grab my keys.

"I'll get it." Logan stands and takes the keys from my hands. When our fingers touch, he holds mine for a moment.

Electric pulses travel from my fingers to my toes at the slight contact, but I don't move my hand away. I lean into it and breathe in the warm citrus smell that mixes with the light scent of wood dust. "Thank you," I tell him. I don't want to risk running him off again.

He grunts in response and follows Alice to my car. I watch from the windows as he secures the car seat beside Zoey's in the back of Alice's SUV. Alice goes around to check it while I give Mia a last list of instructions.

"Baby," I say. "It's been a while since you've had a sleepover. Listen to Zoey's mom and dad, and if you need anything, you just call me. Okay? You'll be good?"

Mia grabs me in a tight hug. "I will. I promise. Love you." And then she, her backpack, sleeping bag, and her new best friend are tearing down the front lawn toward Alice's car.

I watch them drive away, waving until Logan comes back into the house.

He hands me the keys to the car. "I double-checked the seat," he says.

I nod. "Thank you so much for doing that." I know I could have done it myself, but somehow having Logan here, letting him do something for me, just feels better than words. Better than talking.

By now, it's nearly four, and the afternoon sun has dipped behind the clouds. "I'm going to make some tea," I say. "Do you want some?"

"I'd love that."

I head into the kitchen and start the water to boil. I can hear Logan start to hammer, but then he stops. His footsteps are behind me.

"Birdie?"

I turn toward his voice, so low and insistent.

"Yeah?" I step closer to him, searching his eyes. I'm not sure if he's come for an apology, to talk, or something altogether different, but I'm here for whatever it is.

He holds out a hand to me. "You should wear these. The hammering."

Of course. The earplugs. "Why are you so thoughtful?" I ask. I step close to him and reach out my hand. He sets the earplugs in my palm with his right hand, but his other hand is beneath mine. He closes them together, enveloping my hand in both of his.

"I don't want to make things worse for you," he says quietly. "You've been through enough."

"Are you talking about the headache?" I ask. "Or other things?"

"Everything," he grits out. His eyes are inches from mine, their depths so dark and intense, I feel like I could get lost in them if I keep looking.

But I refuse to look away.

He nods slowly, bringing his forehead to touch mine. "I'm sorry," he whispers. "I wish I were a different man."

"I don't," I tell him.

I bring my hands to his face and angle his head back from mine so I can look into his eyes. I lightly stroke the stubble on his cheeks and chin, and his lips part. I drag my eyes away from his perfect lips and beautiful teeth and meet his eyes.

"If you were a different kind of man, we would never have met." I trail a fingertip along his lower lip, and I can feel his whole body react. It's like my touch has shocked him and every muscle has gone tight.

"Birdie," he whispers.

"Crow," I echo.

"Can I be honest with you?" Logan asks.

"I would love that," I say. "You can tell me anything."

"Anything?" he asks. "You're sure?"

I nod, braced for whatever is coming. I'm oddly not nervous or scared. I don't feel like there's anything he could tell me that wouldn't bring me closer to him. I want to grab him and bring our foreheads back together, so I can smell him and feel him as we talk, but what we just shared feels so intimate, I don't know if I should push for more.

Logan steps close to me and puts two fingers under my chin. "Birdie," he breathes, "your sweet tea is kind of awful. And I've been to prison, so that's saying something."

I'm shocked at first, a hand over my mouth. But then I'm laughing. Laughing so hard tears gather in the corners of my eyes. Then Logan is laughing, and before I know it, I'm reaching for him, pulling his face close to mine.

When I lift my lips, he's there, ready for me. His lips touch mine, and the sensation is light and soft, like he's tasting something he's unsure about, but then quickly, the kiss grows dark and intense, like him. I open my mouth, and his tongue tangles with mine. My breath quickens, and liquid heat surges through my core. But he pumps the brakes on the kiss, pulling back reluctantly, slowly. Nibbling my lower lip and arcing a hand beneath my hair to hold the back of my neck.

"Birdie," he breathes.

"Mmm?"

"There's more I need to tell you."

11

CROW

"Can we talk later?" Birdie's rain-cloud eyes are half closed. Her lips are parted, her breath coming in small gasps. "I just want…this. You."

All the plans in my head about what I was going to say, everything I was going to explain, fly out the window. I slide my hands under her hair and weave my fingers through the silky strands. As I touch her, I can smell the warm heat radiating off her body, her hair, a sweet scent of berry and vanilla. My mouth waters, and I hold her head in my hands, searching her face.

"You want me?" I grunt, not wanting to believe it but desperately needing to. "This?"

I lower my lips to hers and try to memorize every second of this experience. I haven't been with a woman in so long, I know there's no way I want to waste any part of it. I release her hair and run my fingers over her lips, her chin, exploring the tender skin, the soft curves of the most beautiful face I've seen. Not just since before prison. Ever.

Birdie awakens something in me that no other woman has. It's primal and raw, the desire and the drive I have to protect her. To be near her. To be part of whatever life this is she's trying to make. Flawed and funny and real. My blood sizzles through my veins, and I'm like a starving man set before a feast, but I refuse to dive in. I need to take my time. This is a moment I didn't realize I've been wanting, and now that it's here, I'm going to make it last.

Birdie isn't a meal. She's nourishment, sustenance. I want to feed off this sweetness as long as I can.

I lower my head and claim her lips in light, fluttering kisses.

"So good," I groan. "You taste so, so good. Feel so, so good."

Her hands are on my back, tentative at first, but as I open my mouth and deepen the kiss, her fingers are searching, pulling me closer. Our hips are pressed together, the heat of our bodies forming a seal I don't ever want to break.

I dip my tongue against hers, then go deeper, our teeth clacking as electricity makes my body tight and hard in all the right places. I scrape my stubble against her chin, her cheeks, and pull back to kiss the tender pink skin of her neck. She's flushed with arousal, her eyes closed, her head thrown back. I trace a line down her throat with my lips, but I stop when I reach the hollow of her neck.

I have to stop. My body is like an animal on the prowl, and I've got Birdie in my sights. I want to claim her, own her, make her mine, but not like this. Not today. Not when there's so much she needs to understand. I could fuck her and run, break the seal on seven long years of celibacy and isolation, but that's not what I want from her. She's not a one-and-done woman. I don't think I'm a one-and-done man anymore. I'm different, and that makes this all the more important.

I don't want things to go so far that neither one of us has taken the time to be sure this is where we want to be. I ease my head back and put the tiniest bit of space between us.

"You're so...*gorgeous*," I breathe, my fingertips worshipping her face, her cut eyebrow, her lips. "Birdie..."

She swallows hard. "Crow... What is this?"

I take in a deep breath of air, but it only brings her intoxicating scent deeper into my senses. If I could get drunk on this woman, I'd be trashed. It's like my body is already wasted, but I'm insatiable, still wanting more.

I grab her hand and lead her out of the kitchen, away from the small space where our bodies are pressed dangerously close. We sit on the couch side by side, and she laces her fingers through mine.

"Crow, I'm—"

"Don't," I tell her. "You don't have to say anything."

"Please," she says. "I'd like to say something. Ask you something, rather."

I nod and tighten my hold on her hand.

"Will you tell me? About yourself? Not just about...*that*. I want to know who you are." She's looking at me with such openness and sincerity it about tears my heart in two. I don't know that I've had a woman ask me that, want to know who I am. The fact that she's asking me this, even though she's fully aware that every word out of my mouth has the potential to disappoint her... That what I tell her could put the pieces of my life together in such a way that I don't turn out to be a man she could want...

It's a risk I have to take. There can't be any lies between us. There's no sugarcoating this reality.

What I felt in her kitchen just now, I want that again. I want more, so much more. I want her, everything about her, from her sore head to her stressed-out heart. I can only hope what I tell her doesn't stop her from ever wanting the same with me. But like everything else I've lived through, there's no way around it. No shortcut. I have to face it and take the fallout, whatever it is.

"I grew up in a military family," I say. "Dad got

moved around a lot. Never in one place for long. Wish I could say my pops was a real American hero, but for him, the military was a job. A lifestyle that fit his rigid view of the world. Right was right, wrong was wrong. People were heroes or devils, and there wasn't any in-between."

"He tried to raise us to be just like him, but…" I chuckle and look down at my arms. "The first time I saw a tattoo on a guy's arm, my destiny changed course pretty quick."

"Yeah?" She curls her feet beneath her and leans against my side. "How so?"

"I wanted ink. I wanted it so badly. To make my body look the way I wanted it to… It felt like an act of definition. I could be what I wanted to be. But my old man saw it as an act of defiance. Told me if I ever got one, I'd be out on the street the same day."

"Did you get one anyway?" she asks, a sly grin on her face.

I nod. "It was a small one, and shit, did it suck." I untangle our hands and lift the hem of my jeans and show her a tiny motorcycle on the inside of my left ankle. The blue-black ink is faded now, but you can still make out what it is. My first. "Dad didn't see this for years. I mean years. It wasn't like he did full-body inspections, and I wasn't exactly a guy who wore khaki shorts, if you know what I mean."

She giggles and runs her fingers along my hairy ankle, tracing the outline of the bike. "So, you've always wanted to ride?" she asks.

"I've always wanted to be free," I tell her. "As fucking corny as it sounds, anything that put space between the oppressive shit my dad spouted off and me, I wanted. Craved. I didn't care what it was—booze, babes, bikes. I wanted to live."

"Babes," she repeats, but she doesn't sound jealous or upset. She's looking at me and reaches a hand to stroke my chin. "I'll bet you had so many girlfriends."

I chuckle. "Not gonna lie. I did well with the ladies. Ironically, I think it's because of how I was raised. I was always honest with chicks. Maybe brutally so. I wanted sex, I told them. If I wanted more, I was straight up about that too. I learned at a young age that women aren't as complicated as guys make them out to be. Be honest with them. It really boils down to that. They can take you or leave you, but only if they know the deal."

She nods. "God, yes. Relationships would be so much easier if men just told the truth." I hear bitterness there that I'm sure she earned the hard way. Through experience.

"I didn't mean to be dishonest with you, Birdie." I clear my throat and rub at my face. "It's not like I was holding something back intentionally."

"Oh God, no, Crow. I didn't mean you—"

"No, no. It's okay. I've only been out a little over a month. I was planning on saying something if you seemed in any way interested in me, but I just haven't had much practice talking about this with people who don't already know. And with you having a kid and all…" I sigh. "I wanted to get those stairs finished so I knew you'd be safe. Just in case you never wanted to speak to me again."

"Crow…"

I take her face between my hands and look into her eyes. "I promise you this, Birdie. I was going to tell you. And I'd like to tell you now."

She blinks, and I see a shimmer of tears in those slate-gray eyes. She nods. "Go ahead."

I drop my hands into my lap and get it all out in a rush before I lose my nerve.

"I was at a bar. I was supposed to meet a chick, but she never showed. I was feeling ornery and drank a few more than I should have. Was just minding my own business, drowning my sorrows, when some guy who was clearly on something started harassing a couple kids playing pool. This was a real redneck hole-in-the-wall dive bar, and these two preppies…" I sigh. "They stuck out like sore thumbs, Birdie. At first, I thought the guy was trying to hustle them, but I don't really know what happened. Things got out of hand fast, and before I knew what was happening, the guy was accusing the preppies of stealing his money."

I close my eyes. I can still picture the guy to this day. It's a face I've actively tried not to think about at times. At other times, it's the only face I see whether I'm awake or sleeping. The beady, bloodshot eyes. The angry mouth, his stained teeth exposing too much of his gums. His dirty shirt and the way his hair was so greasy, I could smell it.

"I was never someone to back down from a fight, but stepping up to join one… That wasn't me either. Maybe I was surly because I'd been stood up, or it was the extra couple drinks, but I got involved."

I shake my head. "The specifics beyond that don't matter. Punches were thrown, but that little tweaker was no match for me. I got a little shitty with him. Called him some names. Tried to embarrass him. I thought maybe he'd leave, but he doubled down. Grabbed a pool stick and hit me with it. After that, I just saw red. I was done with the bullshit and the posturing. I hit him right in the jaw, sent him sailing. He didn't even try to break his fall. Paramedics pronounced him dead at the scene."

I can't say I feel sadness retelling the story. I do feel sick. Uncomfortable. I hate that this one random day, a day when I might have just as easily ended up in bed with Vicky—a girl whose name I only remember because I had to give it to the cops, everything changed because of a series of random choices. And me trying to be a hero without even meaning to.

"The bartenders and witnesses all told the same story, but the facts were the facts. I'd antagonized the guy. Tried to shame him into leaving. Even after everything he did to start it—he threw the punch, the pool stick, all that shit—I was the one who hit a guy and ended his life. Somebody had to pay."

I look down at Birdie, silent tears staining her face.

"I'm sorry," I say again, so quietly I'm not sure who I'm apologizing to. "I'm sorry for what happened to him, to me. All of it."

She wraps her arms around me and holds me tighter than I think I've ever been held before. She rocks slightly, stroking my back and neck, and I close my eyes, trying to banish the name and face of the man I killed that day.

"Can I ask another question?" she says softly, her lips pressing into my shoulder.

"Yeah. Go ahead." I've come this far. I might as well get it all out of the way. If we go any further, I want to know there are no secrets between us.

"Did he...have a family?"

I nod. "Elderly parents," I say. "They came to the trial. They were all he had. Thank God for small favors, in some ways. I can't even imagine if he'd had kids or a wife some place. As it was, I was lucky the parents didn't sue me for damages. Did you know that? They could have sued me for compensation for being responsible." I shake my head. "Anyway, I got less than the full sentence because of the 'undisputed facts.' Everyone agreed that the guy started it. Threw the first punch, hit me with the stick. You know the rest. It was just bad luck for him. The fact that I was big and not a fellow cracked-out, skinny druggie led to things going so badly for him."

I pull away from Birdie's hug. I want to see her eyes when I ask her this question. "Birdie," I whisper, "I'd never hurt anyone like that on purpose. I didn't mean for that to happen. I'm not a violent man. I don't have anger issues. I served my full sentence. Paid my debt. But that doesn't mean I expect you to be able to trust me. Accept me. I won't hold it against you if you don't want me around you and your daughter. Just say the word, and if you want, I'll go. No questions asked."

She pulls my face to hers and kisses my eyes, the tip of my nose, and the scruff on my chin. Her tears wet my face, and she pulls away, holding up a finger. "I need a tissue, or we're going to be swapping more than just tears."

She trots off to the half-bath off the kitchen and returns blowing her nose, a wad of tissues in one hand. She sits back beside me and grabs one of my hands. She laces our fingers together and looks down at our hands.

"My life is…" She laughs, a dry, sad sound. "…a goddamn mess. I'm a now-unemployed single mom. My house is a wreck, my body is falling to bits." She shakes her head. "My mom held our lives together with love and hard work. Without her…" Birdie swallows back tears. "It's all been so much to handle. Every day, I wake up feeling like I'm letting everyone down. My daughter. My employer. Former employer, now. Myself."

She looks up at me, her gray eyes stormy. "Crow," she says, "I'm so far from perfect, it's not even funny. I'm holding my life together with tape and prayers. I haven't dated in years—I mean years. And kissing? I haven't been kissed in…too long. And never like that."

I'm looking down at the way she's stroking the wings of the sparrows inked on my hands as we talk.

"I'm sorry I Googled you, but I wanted to know more about the man I'm starting to have feelings for."

"Feelings," I echo. "And how do you feel now?"

She meets my eyes. "My father never married my mother. For years, he stayed with my mom in this very house, part time. He never wanted to give up his own life, his own place. He was a trial lawyer and had a really demanding schedule. At least, that's what he told her." She shakes her head. "That turned out to be total bullshit. Total bullshit. He was married, Crow. The whole time. He had an affair with my mother while he had a wife and three kids at home. The place he went back to when he wasn't here, sleeping with my mother and lying to our faces, was a place he lived with his real family. A family that wasn't us."

I tighten my hold on her and move closer on the couch, our thighs touching. I want to wrap my arms around her, protect her from the pain just talking about this is causing her, but I don't trust myself. I'm wound so tight that if I bring her close, I may not be able to stop myself. And this is not a time for acting on my impulses. She still hasn't told me how she feels about everything I've said, but I don't want to stop her from talking. More than anything, that's what I want. To know her. To hear her. The real Birdie. Just like I hope someday she'll want to know the real me.

"I'm so sorry," I say. "How did your mom find out?"

She takes a deep breath. "One day, I got hurt at day care. It was nothing serious. I tripped and bit down on my lip so hard they thought I might have bit right through it. There was so much blood, the day care staff tried to reach my mom to come get me and take me to a doctor. They couldn't reach her, so they checked my emergency contacts and called my father at his office. Turns out, his secretary was out sick that day. She must have been the gatekeeper of all my dad's secrets. Whoever was covering the desk in her absence told the day care that Dad was at lunch with his wife, but that as soon as he returned, she'd deliver the message.

"When my mom finally got out of her meeting, she came flying over to the day care center. The owner told Mom that she'd left messages for both of my parents, so Mom called my dad's office to let him know she'd made it to me. By then, I was fine. The bleeding had stopped so they knew I had a nice deep cut, but I hadn't bitten through my lip. I was only four, but I remember that day like it was yesterday."

Her fingers stop tracing my bird tattoos as she talks, going deeper and deeper into memory.

"Long story short, the temp told my mom the same thing she told the day care. That Dad was at lunch with his wife. My mom confronted my dad, and he denied it. Over and over and over. But she knew, Crow. All the signs and things she'd ignored or explained away over the five years… She'd seen them all. She just didn't want to believe the truth that was right there."

I want to understand the grief in her eyes, the lost, faraway look on her face. "I'm sorry," is all I can mutter. "For your mother. For you. People can be…shit."

"They can and they are. So many of them. But not you, Crow." She twists a little on the couch, so she's fully facing me while never letting go of my hands. "I'm not going to pretend it's not a big deal. You've got stuff

161

on your record that's going to forever change your life. Voting, credit, buying a house, getting a job. It's complicated, I'm sure. And I don't know any of the details." She sighs, and the depth of her sadness tells me she understands exactly how hard things are going to be.

"But you know what doesn't change?" she asks.

"The way you tease Mia. The way you throw yourself into your work. How thoughtful you are. How you're honest about my sweet tea being shit." She chuckles. "Your father and my father may look perfect on paper, but they don't have a fraction of the heart and soul you do. It just sucks that having a heart like yours has come at such a heavy cost. I can't begin to imagine how you bear it."

She kisses the sparrows on my hands. "I don't want to pretend I get it or that it won't be hard, but I'd like to try. To get to know you. To spend more time with you. I'm not afraid of you or what you've told me. I'm afraid that I can't possibly pull my own weight. No job, my money problems." She shakes her head. "I'm not exactly a fun time. And with my headache issues...I can't make any promises, Crow. All I can offer you is what I have and who I am. And that's all I want from you. We'll figure the rest out as we go."

"You think?" I can't believe what I'm hearing. We're like two birds with clipped wings who've fallen from the nest but have somehow found each other. We might not be able to fly, but we can waddle around. Together.

"I *know*," she breathes.

I grab the back of her neck and bring her face to mine. I fist her hair gently, and a soft moan escapes her lips.

"Too hard?" I ask, lightening my touch.

"No, don't stop. It feels so good."

She shifts her weight so she's straddling my lap. Her nails dig into my shoulders, and she initiates the kiss, as hungry and greedy for me as I am for her. She sweeps the tip of her tongue against my lips, and I open to her, before claiming her mouth with mine. She purrs, a happy, needy sound deep in her throat, and I hold her against me as I let myself get lost in her kiss.

Stars dance behind my eyes, and in this moment, all I feel and taste is Birdie. Her sweetness. Her sorrow. Her joy. It's as if, when we kiss, we connect in a way that surpasses words. I don't have to apologize for who I am. She doesn't have to explain what she doesn't have. It's just raw, honest desire, emotion, and connection between us.

My past fades into the background. It's not gone, but it's not a noose around my neck, holding me back just as I'm close to reaching a goal. Right now, kissing Birdie, I'm freer than I've ever been. And it feels like flying.

I'm kissing her so greedily, I have to come up for

air. But she pushes my chest lightly and rolls her hips against my lap. I close my eyes and let her explore my shoulders with her hands, kneading and stroking the tight muscles. God, I feel like I could explode with pleasure and even pain. My shoulders haven't been touched by anyone in so long, it's like years of pent-up tension start to break loose under her hands.

She must feel my body relaxing because she works her hands around to the back of my neck. She kisses my forehead and pinches the taut cords that line the back of my neck until I'm gasping for relief. It feels so good it hurts, this pleasurable pain. When her nails scratch against my scalp, I feel the sting of tears in my eyes. I'm not even ashamed. I'm so grateful. So fucking grateful to this woman. She explores the landscape of my head with her gentle fingers, scratching and stroking, until I'm panting and so relaxed, I don't know if I'm asleep or in a sensual trance. But this power she has over me is real, and if this is submission, I never want to take back control.

She brings her fingers tenderly to my forehead, where she circles my temples with the pads of her thumbs while leaning close to plant kisses on my face while she massages me. When she stops, her eyes are half closed, her lids heavy and her lips parted.

"My turn," I demand. She's already sitting in my lap, so wrap my arms around her and cuddle her against me. I start off copying her moves, massaging her shoulders and adjusting the pressure based on her happy, contended coos. A little harder, a little softer, I work my way down her back, all the way to the swell of her hips.

She gasps when I knead her ass cheeks, my hands only able to grab the upper part while she's still planted in my lap. "This too much?" I whisper, my voice hoarse and my words hardly more than a whisper.

"No," she says. "Not too much. You're perfect."

I want to keep going. To feel her thighs around my neck, to taste her core, but this is a woman I could build something real with. And I know, now more than ever, that things worth having take time. Time to shape and grow and develop. Like anything I've ever made or fixed with my hands, I know that if I rush this, I'll fuck it up. I just know I will.

Against every desire of my body, I pull my hands from her hips and hold her forehead to mine.

"Birdie," I breathe, my lips inches from hers.

I kiss her again, light kisses that only stoke the flames inside me. But I won't burn the whole place down before I get a chance to learn how to control this heat. I kiss her again and again until, finally, I say, "I think I need to cool off... How about I make us some sweet tea?"

She drops her head to my shoulder and laughs.

When she lifts her face to mine, her eyes are dilated, the gray now almost completely consumed by black.

"Crow," she breathes my name, and it sounds so right coming from her lips, deep pink and swollen from my teeth and kisses. "I would love that."

BIRDIE

"Mom. Mama."

I sit up as my bedroom door flies open. Mia launches herself onto my bed, knocking one of my pillows onto the floor. "Whoa, baby. Slow down."

The sun is barely up, but I know Mia probably didn't sleep a wink all night. And not because she'd been having nightmares. It's Saturday, and today Mia, Crow, and I are going to that baby shower together. It's been a long and winding week, full of stolen kisses, heated texts, and, oddly, a new kind of intimacy forged through routine.

Crow's been using my car all week, coming by early to pick up Mia to drive her to school. I tag along, and after, he comes back to my place to work on some kind of project on the house. In a week's time, he's redone my stairs, hung a handrail, and he's now working on a cosmetic renovation of my powder room. That toilet and sink are original to the house, and while they both work okay, swapping them out for more efficient appliances and giving the room a little facelift will look great on Crow's resume.

I've been job-hunting and trying to sort out health insurance and doctor visits, all of which is a full-time job in and of itself.

Crow and I agreed to take things slow between us, so the week has been full of touching, kissing, and a lot of taking care of my needs privately after Crow goes home and Mia is in bed, if you know what I mean.

"Mama, we need to make a plan for what we're going to buy the baby."

Mia has been dying to go to the store and shop for baby presents, but that's been another stress on my mind. Discretionary spending gives me a stomachache. Alice knows I've lost my job, and she's assured me that Lia and Leo, their friends who are expecting the baby, won't even notice if I don't bring anything. She suggested I bake some cupcakes instead, but after Crow very gently suggested we *not* bring anything home-made, I got the message. I've never been a good cook or baker, and giving the baby shower guests food poisoning would be worse than showing up empty-handed.

I sit up and tug Mia close. "You can pick out one

thing at the store, okay? I don't want you going bananas, little miss."

"I promise, no bananas." She skips off to her room to pick out an outfit while I head downstairs to make coffee.

The last week, my headaches haven't been anywhere near as frequent as they were before my trip down the stairs. I don't want to draw any faulty conclusions. It's possible that being happier, even though my stress level is not much lower, is helping dial back the frequency and intensity of the episodes.

But I don't want to fool myself into thinking a new relationship is the cure. Stress makes my head worse, but it didn't create the condition. I still need to figure out getting in to see people and navigating the maze of insurance questions, especially now that my insurance is set to expire in a couple of days.

But those are worries for tomorrow. Today, I'm going to meet more of Crow's friends. My little girl is going to play with her new best friend. And maybe, just maybe, this will be the night that Crow sleeps over.

I try not to get ahead of myself, but I shower and shave, pluck and primp every inch of my body. Mia is knocking on the bathroom door before long, asking if she can have a special hairstyle for the baby shower.

By the time we're both dressed and ready, there's a knock at the door, and Mia, if possible even more excited than she was when she woke up, flies to answer it.

"Mia. Wait for me," I remind her.

I check the peephole, and my breath catches when I see Crow standing there. I twist the lock, and Mia yanks open the door.

"Crow," she greets him and grabs his hand. "Come in. I have a lot of ideas about the baby gift." She drags him inside, talking a blue streak.

As he walks past me, Crow reaches out a hand to me, and I grab it. We hold hands for a moment, and then, like lovestruck teenagers, giggle and let each other go.

Mia doesn't know there's anything going on between Crow and me. For now, he's a good friend helping with projects at the house and driving her to school while I'm limiting my time behind the wheel. I've never brought anyone home to meet Mia, so I don't know exactly how to navigate that terrain. I'm sure when the time is right, I'll figure it out, but since it's early, I figure I can keep this close to my heart, at least as far as my daughter is concerned.

We head out to the store and let Mia run through the infant aisles, making lists in her head of things she'd like to get. I told her she can pick three things, and we'll choose only one to buy and take to the baby, so she's very seriously considering what her top three choices are.

Crow and I wander the "boring" aisle, browsing the infant formula and bottles while Mia heads straight for the toys. Once we're alone, I lean close to his ear.

Crow's wearing a shirt I've never seen him in before. A blue button-down with a pair of black jeans. His hair is styled, swept back from his face and held into place with a light gel or something. His glossy hair is so dark, it suits his nickname perfectly. I breathe the stronger aroma of aftershave, the now-familiar scents of citrus and wood making my knees weak and my core run lava-hot.

"Hi, sexy." I lightly kiss his ear, and he shudders visibly. "You look gorgeous today."

"Woman," he growls. "This is a place to shop for babies, not to make 'em."

"Shop for baby *stuff*," I tease. I lace my fingers through his, kiss the pretty bird on his hand, and then release him. "I'm looking forward to meeting your friends today," I tell him. "Will it be a lot of bikers?"

He nods. "I expect the whole crew'll be there." He chuckles. "This is definitely not the club parties I expected to come back to."

He tucks two fingers under my chin and just looks at me when Mia comes running down the aisle. "Mama. Crow. Look."

I expect Mia to have all three things she wants us to choose from, but to my surprise, she's only got one thing in her hand.

"This," she says, thrusting a box at me. "It's so cute."

I take the box from her, and as I'm inspecting the contents, it hits me how absolutely perfect this gift really is.

"Honey," I ask her. "Do you know what this is?"

She nods. "Yeah, of course I do. It's a giraffe." She looks up at Crow and smiles. "The baby will have one just like mine."

The giraffe isn't exactly like Mia's. It's a smaller version, and it's called a binkie buddy. The giraffe itself is super soft, and it's built to connect to a pacifier so the baby can hold on to something while the binkie is in their mouth. As the infant gets older, the connective strap converts and can clip to a car seat or stroller, even a backpack. And to my surprise, the gift is even less than I expected to spend. My heart nearly breaks not only at the fact that I can spend under what I'd budgeted, but that the gift is so perfectly meaningful to us.

I kneel down and look my daughter in the eye. "Honey, this is perfect. This is what you want to get?"

She looks up at Crow and takes the box from me,

extending it for him to inspect. "What do you think?" she asks.

He presses his lips together for a moment. "You know what the worst part about being a giraffe is?" he asks.

She shakes her head.

"The sore throats," he says seriously.

Mia cracks up and turns back to me. "So, can we get it?"

I nod. "Let's find a card so you can explain why you picked it. That will make the gift even more special."

She leaves the box with me and darts off to look for a card. She's already reading at grade level with the kids in second grade, so I leave her to pick out whatever card she wants.

"Seems like you've made quite an impression on both of us," I say quietly.

"I might need to buy Mia a new stuffed animal," he admits. "There are only so many giraffe jokes on the internet."

I lace my fingers through his until we're in sight of Mia. She's got her face pressed close to the cards to read what they say, but when she sees us approach, she picks one out and we pay for the gift. On the drive to the shower, I let Mia assemble the gift in the gift bag we picked out.

I'm oddly excited to meet Crow's friends. These

people are more his family than his biological relatives, and if Alice and Morris are anything to judge by, I'm going to have a great day.

As soon as we park, Mia takes off running.

"I swear," I tell him, "my daughter is not normally a roadrunner, racing from A to B."

He holds the gift bag while I climb out of the car, then he hands the bag to me to carry. "Mind if I add my card to your bag?" he asks. "I got them an, uh, evergreen gift..."

I chuckle and slide his card inside the gift bag just as Zoey runs out to greet Mia. The girls head into the house, and we follow close behind.

The next few minutes are a whirlwind of introductions. Alice greets me first, giving me a huge hug.

"How are you?" she asks. "You look fantastic." She points to my eyebrow but then looks me over from head to toe. "Poor Crow," she says, shaking her head. "Or should I say lucky?"

I flush and shake off the compliment. "How are you?" I ask, lowering my voice. "Do you want any help?"

"Nope. Everything here is done. Come on, let me introduce you to everyone. Are you okay with dogs?"

"Do you have dogs? Mia is going to lose it." The only thing my daughter wants more than siblings and friends is a puppy.

"Not ours," she explains. "Lia, the mommy-to-be, has a whole pack of them. They're all very friendly, though."

I can hear dogs barking outside and Mia squealing, which means she's already met the pups. Alice leads me into the backyard, where the party is already in full swing. An enormous man is sitting in an Adirondack chair, a beer in his hands.

Mia and Zoey are running around chasing dogs, and a very pretty, very pregnant girl in a boho-style maxi dress is barefoot as she sits and talks to two very, very handsome guys.

"Birdie," Alice says. She stops first in front of the giant man. "This is Tiny, president of the motorcycle club and Lia's dad."

Tiny grunts, and Crow lets out a belly laugh. "Come on, old man." He holds out a hand and yanks Tiny up from the chair.

"Nice to meet you," Tiny says, holding out a hand to me. "I hear you're risking your house so Crow over here can put together a résumé of construction projects. I don't know whether to feel sorry for you or thank you."

I shake his hand and look at Crow, who's shaking his head. He flicks Tiny on the shoulder and hisses, "Asshole." But the grins on their faces let me know the ribbing is well-intentioned.

"Congratulations," I say, then Alice whisks me off to meet the guest of honor and the guys she's chatting up.

"Lia," Alice interrupts. "There's someone here I want you to meet."

Lia stands up, huffing a breath from the exertion. "No, no, no," she exclaims. "I want to meet you. Are you Mia's mom? Because all I have heard about for the last few weeks is Mia this, Mia that. Zoey's already planning all the ways your daughter is going to help her babysit this little egg." She rubs her belly.

I give her a hug and wish her congratulations, a tiny spark of longing filling my chest. I'm not jealous. But I never had a shower like this, loved ones and friends and dogs and happiness spilling over. While Mom and I were overjoyed with Mia once she arrived, the pregnancy wasn't something we really had time to celebrate.

"Come on," Lia says, walking over to the two gorgeous men talking in low voices. "Meet the baby daddy. This is Leo."

Leo greets me, and I recognize him as the newest member of the motorcycle club, from what Crow has told me. Crow and Leo clasp arms in a warm bro-hug, but I notice a definite chill when Crow greets the other guy.

"And this is Arrow," Alice says.

Arrow doesn't look like the other guys. He's smoother, more refined in a way, even though colorful tattoos line his well-defined arms. While the other guys have a relaxed, almost rowdy air about them, Arrow is more reserved.

"Glad to see you, man," he says, holding out his hand to Crow.

There's a lot to interpret in their greeting, and I'm hoping I'll get the lowdown from Crow later. Before I know what's happening, there are more introductions, Tim and Juliette, Leo's brother and his girlfriend, and a few more guys with names like Dog and Eagle.

The backyard is colorfully decorated with streamers and balloons, and the cake is a work of art. Crow and I eat and talk, and I enjoy the company of these friendly strangers.

As the sun starts to sink in the sky, Alice sidles up to me and puts an arm over my shoulders. "Soooo," she says, a grin on her face. "How would you feel about leaving your little angel here for a sleepover? Mia and Zoey haven't left each other's side all afternoon. Between chasing and feeding the dogs, they haven't been inside at all, and I bet after all this running, they'll actually sleep."

"Alice," I say, "are you up for an overnight guest? You have all this cleaning to do, and..." I don't say it out loud since I know she and Morris were holding on to the news about their baby until after this shower.

She shakes her head. "Tiny's already got the guys on

it. I won't have much to do but supervise. And honestly, it'll be great for Morris and me. I can put my feet up and relax and know that Zoey's not bored. Besides—" she gives me a sisterly nudge in the shoulder "—if you're feeling up to a date night…"

I brush the hair away from my face. "It is that obvious?"

"Honey, I know you and Crow came here together, but he's been looking at you all afternoon like he can't wait to leave with you." Alice's words are teasing but sincere.

I look over at Crow, who hasn't been out of my line of sight all afternoon. He's chatting with Arrow, a thoughtful, almost dark look on his face. I'll have to ask him what the deal is later. Even though he looks deep in conversation, he glances up and sees me watching him, and the corner of his mouth curves into a smile. The darkness of his gaze lightens a bit. Even Arrow notices the change and follows Crow's eyes to me.

Arrow nods and claps Crow on the shoulder, then walks away to talk to Tim.

"If you're sure…" I say. "Will you call me if it's too much? If she's up late or anything? What about dinner? Can I give you some money for food?"

"Are you serious? We have enough of these left-overs to feed the whole club." Alice swats my arm and shoves me toward Crow. "Zoey!" she yells. "How would you like Mia to sleep over tonight?"

The girls' response is predictable—excitement mixed with begging.

"No, Zoey. Absolutely not." Alice shakes her head before they get too carried away. "Lia's dogs are going home with her. You know Dad's rules. No dogs inside the house."

"Aw..." Zoey's only momentarily discouraged by that, but then Mia runs up to me.

"Mama, we didn't pack anything for a sleepover. I don't have a toothbrush or pajamas."

"We have extras," Alice assures us. "You don't need a thing unless your mom says you do."

Once we work out the logistics, we start the process of saying our goodbyes. That takes a solid half hour, even with Crow abruptly cutting short the hugs and nice-to-meet-yous. After a last goodbye hug to Mia with reminders to mind Alice and to call if she needs anything, Crow and I walk through the house and toward my car.

The whole night is ahead of us. And we get to spend it however we want.

BACK AT MY PLACE, I start to fade fast.

"Hey." Crow walks me to the front door, but he hesitates as I unlock it. "You look exhausted, Birdie. I don't have to come in. You have the night off. You should rest if you need it."

I open the door and loop my hand through his arm. "Get your hot ass in here." I lock the door and drop my purse and keys. "I could use a little rest, for sure. Today was awesome, but I'm feeling it. A lot of activity, a lot of stimulation. Mind if we chill on the couch a bit?"

He shakes his head. "I'll get drinks. You want sweet tea?" he asks.

"Only if you make it," I reply.

He chuckles and takes a few minutes in the kitchen while I get comfy on the couch. I close my eyes and think through all the people I met today. None of them were what I expected. Lia and Leo are so adorable, so touchy-feely and so completely in love. Dog and Eagle and Tiny are brawny bikers, but sitting around drinking beer and eating puppy-themed cupcakes, they seemed nothing like what I imagined Crow's biker brothers would be.

There was only one person at that party who gave me pause in any way.

"Here ya go." Crow sets two tall glasses filled to the brim on the coffee table, then joins me on the couch.

He sits in the position I've come to expect, his legs spread open and stretched along the length of the couch.

I tuck in between his legs and rest the back of my head against his chest. I close my eyes while he strokes my temples.

"So," I start. "What's the deal with you and Arrow? Every time you talked to him today, you seemed…uncomfortable."

I can feel Crow take a big breath of air and then slowly release it.

"That bad?" I chuckle. I keep my eyes closed, giving myself a little time to wind down while I run my hands over the black denim that covers his muscular thighs.

"Nah, it ain't bad," he says. "Arrow wants me to come work for him."

I nod slightly, intensifying the pressure of my fingertips on his legs. "Good thing? Bad thing? Fill me in?"

Another of those deep-chested sighs before he says, "Little of both. He used to be a bail agent but now is a private investigator. Running down insurance scammers and cheating spouses." The gentle pressure of his hands on my scalp intensifies just a bit as he talks. "I don't know. The money would be good, and obviously, that'd be good for me, for us. But something about ratting people out, spending my days digging up dirt on people doing shady shit…"

"It sounds a lot like being a cop or law enforcement," I say. "But without the police powers."

"Shit…" He sounds surprised, and I turn to look at

him. "Birdie, do you think that's it? I've been racking my brain to figure out what the big deal is. It's not illegal, it's not immoral. He gets paid by clients for information they need. It shouldn't be a problem, but every time I think about doing it, my gut just…" He shrugs.

"Could be," I say gently. "After what you've been through, I could see you feeling a lot of things. Fear, hesitation. In some ways, you'd be putting yourself in the position of power over people who, I don't know… Maybe are people whose circumstances you can relate to a little too closely. I can see why you're torn."

He lowers his head so his chin rests lightly on the top of my head. "This makes a hell of a lot of sense. I don't know why I didn't see it that way. It's good money, though, babe."

"Babe?" I wiggle from under the gentle weight of his head and face him. "I like how that sounds."

"Better than Birdie?" he asks, smiling.

"I like it all," I admit. I lean forward and give him a light kiss on the cheek, not ready to end the conversation just yet. "Money is only one reason to take work," I remind him. "If it doesn't feel right, you shouldn't feel pressure to do it."

"I don't," he admitted. "I told him I'd give it a try this week. Just one assignment to see how it feels. He's going to give me a car to use. I guess he's got an agreement with a rental company. He prefers not to use his own truck when he's watching people or running around, so he'll give the same to me while I'm working."

"Is that what you want? Are you really okay with this?" I don't have solutions to his problems, and I really don't want him to feel like anything I'm going through should factor into his decisions. If he wants my car, it's his. Other than taking Mia to and from school, which I'm fully cleared to do now, I have no place to be next week.

"It is," he says. "The money will help a lot, and who knows. Maybe I can do it short-term. Until I get the construction stuff off the ground."

He sounds okay with it, but I'm not sure. I decide not to press him. He knows what he can and cannot stomach. I leave him with one last thought.

"Crow," I say, "I'm really glad you're thinking about options for the future, but I had a more short-term project I was hoping to get your help with."

He cocks his chin, those dark-chocolate eyes staring through to my soul. "Yeah? What'd you have in mind?"

"I've got this itch I just can't scratch," I say quietly.

"Want me to try to find it?" he asks, his voice every bit as low as mine.

"Please?"

He puts his hands on my hips and guides me back into the position I was in before, tucked in between the length of his legs. I lean my back against his chest and close my eyes.

"Is it here?" he asks, trailing his fingers along the tops of my shoulders.

"No," I whisper, my voice growing husky. "Keep trying."

"Here?" He's stroking my arms, his large hands sliding over my skin. I look down at those perfect sparrows on his hands as they flutter down my body.

"Nuh-huh," I say.

"Any place I can't check?" he rasps. I can feel him hardening behind me, and I stifle a thrilled grin at the way his body responds to me.

"Babe. I'm all yours."

He groans softly but keeps the pace light and the pressure even. He works his fingertips into my shoulders and trails his fingers gently over the front of my throat before working his way down to the front of my blouse. I arch my back slightly, my nipples aching with need. He traces his fingertips over the hard tips so lightly I can hardly feel anything but a tease. I squirm as heat floods my core, and I strain against my blouse, desperate for more.

"Birdie." His breath is hot against my ear as he cups my breasts in his hands. "Do you like this?"

"God yes," I breathe.

It's not a matter of liking anything.

When he circles the weight of my breasts with his hands, his fingers pinching and twisting my nipples, I start to come undone. My mouth opens, and I'm breathing fast, need and arousal making everything cloudy. I throw my head back against his chest and give in to the sensation, losing all sense of time and space. My body, so often my enemy, takes over, pleasure spreading through my limbs. I wiggle my hips, trying to get closer to him, and I hold my hands over his, increasing the exquisite pressure on my breasts.

"Birdie…" His breaths are coming heavy now too, and the tension I feel against my back grows to an uncomfortable point.

"Crow," I huff. "Let's take this upstairs."

CROW

I FOLLOW BIRDIE UPSTAIRS. MY THOUGHTS ARE RACING, but the tsunami in my chest is more than just fear and anxiety. Unlike in the past when I was content to get off and get a girl off, this isn't like those other times. This is about so much more. This is about Birdie. About us.

I can't overthink things for too long, though, because by the time we get to the top of the stairs, Birdie is reaching for my hand and dragging me into her room.

"Are you okay?" she asks. "Is this too soon?"

"Too soon?" I shake my head, emotions crashing in my chest like waves on a stormy sea. "Baby, I feel like I've waited a lifetime for you."

We stand beside her bed, just looking at each other. I reach for her hand and pull her close. She tucks her head against my chest, and I just breathe in the scent of her.

"Crow," she whispers. "I-I have to bring something up…"

"What?" I growl, but it's restrained. My sense of protectiveness for this woman takes over. As much as I want her for myself, I pull back and look into her eyes, concern warring with the excitement of anticipation and desire. "What is it? Do you have a headache? Because we can stop—"

"No." Her smile is a little shy. "It's been so long, I don't even know if I have condoms in the house. If I do, they're probably so old they're brittle."

My shoulders relax and I nod. *Right.* And also, shit.

"That's okay," I tell her. "I was tested for everything under the sun when I was inside. Haven't been with anyone but my right hand in years. I'm okay without if you are." I can't deny I want her. Badly enough to be reckless? Enough to make short-term decisions with long-term consequences? This is one time, one situation where I'm going to follow someone else's lead. "Birdie?" I whisper. "This is all you. What do you want?"

"God, I want you," she sighs, dropping her forehead against my chest. Her words are soft but clear. "It's the pregnancy thing," she says. "I've got a one-for-one track record getting knocked up when I'm even the tiniest bit careless."

Mia… Right, of course. "Okay. What do you want to do?" I ask.

She fists my shirt and tugs my face close to hers. Her breath is soft against my lips. "Be creative," she suggests. "Until we have protection."

"I can do creative," I say. I wrap a hand behind her neck and nip her lower lip. "I'll do creative forever if it means being with you."

"Crow?" she gasps, a seductive smile on her lips. "I've been wanting to do this for…maybe since I first met you."

Before I can say anything, how the scent of her has haunted my dreams, how she's the best thing about being free again, the only thing I look forward to and the reason I can climb out of bed in the morning and face the bullshit and beauty of another day, Birdie is unfastening the buttons of my shirt. Her fingers are moving slowly, almost like she's nervous. Every button, every inch, my heart is pounding harder in my chest, until I'm sure she'll be able to feel the beat through my skin.

When she finally tugs the fabric over my arms and drops it on the bedside table, she looks at my chest for a moment, a girlish grin on her face. She trails her fingers over my pecs, the sensation sending shock waves of heat through my body.

"You're fucking hot," she says. "Phew."

I shake my head, but my grin's stretching from ear to ear. "Look who's talking," I mutter, but the words fade into a heated moan when she plants her lips on my sternum.

She kisses from my pecs to my stomach, her lips soft and her breath hot. She trails the tip of her tongue along my skin, and while it should cool me, her touch sends my body into overdrive. I'm hot, I'm shaking, and I'm in danger of losing control. Every flick of her tongue feels so, so good, and she's pushing me onto the bed so she can taste more of my skin with her mouth.

I'm lying on my back, my legs spread wide, and all I can see is Birdie. Birdie's arms braced on the bed as she kisses every inch of my torso and belly. Birdie's smile as she straddles my hips and leans close to tap my nose with hers.

"God, Crow, you taste so delicious," she croons, before crushing my mouth with hers.

This kiss is frantic, a desperate, hungry tangle of tongues and lips, our teeth tapping against each other as we deepen the kiss. My hands fisting her hair, her hands cradling the sides of my face so we're connected in every possible way we can touch each other until we have to break apart, breathless and needing air.

"Crow," she pants. Her lips are swollen, her chin red from the scrape of my stubble against her. "I want you so bad."

I flip her onto her back, tugging her blouse away and tossing it aside a lot less carefully than she did mine.

"Sorry," I pant, "I don't have your patience."

I stare down at her, her dark hair spilling over the pillows, her stormy eyes clearer than I've ever seen them. Her nipples are so hard they look like they're going to cut through the nearly transparent fabric of her bra, and for a moment, I just look at her. I don't touch, but I savor the woman she is. Her beauty. Her trust.

We're in a nearly dark room, the little light there is allowing me to see how much this woman wants me. Just like I want her. We're safe. We have a roof over our heads. And there's nothing to do but pleasure each other. Learn each other's secrets. All the ones we haven't yet been able to share.

I don't have the words for the storm of emotions and sensations fighting in my body and heart to take over, but it turns out, I don't need to say or do a thing. Birdie arches her back and reaches behind her to unfasten the clasp on her bra. She's shoving the straps down her arms and saying, "I'm so glad we met, Crow. Who would have thought one of the hardest days of my life so far would bring me one of the best things that's ever happened?"

"Me?" I grit out.

My heart would probably explode even if she

weren't bare before me, her full breasts and nipples hard and looking sweet enough to eat.

"You," she confirms.

I lower my head and draw one nipple into my mouth, slowly working my tongue over the hard tip. The taste of her is better than the sweetest juice, more powerful than the burn of the best whiskey I've ever sipped. She is heat and light, fire and sweetness, and I work her peaks with my mouth like her body itself can give me life.

She squirms and gasps with pleasure, and I respond to her every movement and moan, flicking and sucking until she's scratching my back and pushing her chest against me. She tears her fingers through my hair and pulls my face impossibly close to her breast. I kiss the fullness of it, nip the peak with my teeth, suck as much of the plush fullness into my mouth, every sound she makes like gasoline thrown on my fire.

I stop to claim her mouth again, sending my fingers on a journey to unfasten her pants. She kisses me back roughly, sitting up and helping me undo the belt and zipper. She leans back, and I wrestle the denim so I can see her, all of her. Her panties come away with the jeans, so she's lying on her back fully naked, her legs slightly shaking and her breasts bright pink from the rough love of my chin and teeth and lips. What I wouldn't do to feast on her this way every day. Always.

There are no limits, no resistance with Birdie. She wants me as much as I want her, the desire emanating from her in waves.

"Anything off-limits?" I grit out. I want to learn her pleasure, every twist and stroke and lick and how to dial into her desire, but that's gonna take time. Before we even start the trip, I wanna know where the boundaries are.

"I'm yours," she whispers. "Anything you want."

My entire body starts to vibrate like a plucked string at her open invitation. I soak up her body first with my eyes. Her thighs, her knees slightly together, the long, slim muscles tense as she curls her hands into the sheet. If her body is a banquet, I want to skip everything else and start with the dark mound of curls that sits enticingly like the main course.

Her thighs are hot under my hands as I stroke and knead the skin. I feel my way from the tops of her legs to her knees, cupping the tight muscles of her calves in my palms. I settle between her legs and spread them wide, swallowing the last bit of fear, the last bit of rational thought that's got my mind in a tailspin.

Stop thinking. Just feel.

I start with my fingers, parting the curls and teasing my way lower. Her tiny sighs sound first like surprise and wonder, but they quickly change into heated gasps. I move slowly past the V of her lips, dragging my fingers through her juices. She's so wet, I stroke her folds and dampen my fingertips so that when I find that tight bundle, I can work slippery circles around her bud.

It doesn't take me long to find her sweet spot. She cries out my name and her legs twitch, so I ease back and take my time, drawing lazy circles over her clit. I may have been in a rush to get here, but now that I am, I'm taking my time.

"Crow, oh my God, right there... So good." She starts to work her hips back and forth in time with my touch, so I keep my thumb on her clit to apply a little pressure while I slide my middle finger inside her.

She bucks against my hand, so I swap my thumb for my tongue and lick her clit in time with long, slow strokes along her walls with my fingers.

"Logan," she pants, my real name sounding like a love song on her lips.

Her breath, her cries, the shaking of her entire body when she climaxes, send my body into a frenzy. My dick is so hard, the tip is already weeping, and my balls are tight against my body. While she rides out her orgasm, her legs tight around me, I can taste the peachy-sweet juices of her release on my tongue.

I don't move a muscle, just rest my cheek against her damp thigh, my fingers still planted deep inside her, while she strokes my hair with weak fingers.

She groans when she shifts, trying to sit up. "Well, if that's getting creative… Oh, Crow…"

I climb to the top of the bed and cuddle her to my chest, but she's giving me a sultry look and moving onto her hands and knees. "Snuggle later."

I'm still wearing my jeans and socks, so together, we peel off my clothes and drop them on the floor. In a slow, methodical way, Birdie explores my body with her eyes.

"You have so many more tattoos," she whispers. "So many more stories."

I chuckle. I do, but the way my dick is stabbing the air, I don't think I could answer any questions if she asked them. I don't think I can say my own name when Birdie's hand goes right for my dick. She strokes the shaft, her fingers light, and then she grips it more firmly in her hand and lowers her mouth. When her lips touch the head with hot, breathy kisses and sweet, light licks, the blast of electricity nearly sends my body through the ceiling.

But I quickly adjust to the sensation of her mouth on me. Her soft hair spills over my belly and thighs, and when I can manage to keep my eyes open, I can see her full breasts bounce as she takes my length into her mouth.

I gasp, then utter a stream of curses as her tongue, light and so wet, works around the head, while her hand grips my shaft. I want this to be slow, sexy. I want to take all she's willing to give and then some, but way, way too soon, I'm trembling and warning her she might want to pull away.

But she stays, and I release in her mouth, a sensation so foreign and intense that I lose control of my body. I'm thrashing and moaning, my hands going weak in her hair until, finally, I crash my head back against the wall, dripping sweat and breathless.

She excuses herself to the bathroom and returns just a few moments later. She climbs into bed beside me with a dry hand towel in her hands. She blots my forehead of sweat, then sets the towel aside and cuddles up beside me.

I hold her close, and for long minutes, neither one of us says a word. There's a heat in the air of the room, thick with the scent of our releases but so, so sweet. But the weirdest feeling of all is how familiar it all is. How she feels made to fit against my bare chest, her slim arms perfectly slung over my belly, her damp hair clinging to my skin. She strokes the hair on my belly until her hand goes still. She's dozing quietly, her breathing even, her chest rising and falling in an almost perfect rhythm with mine.

I'm satisfied and happy, my body relaxed and my mind at ease. But despite how perfect this is, how good and safe and free I feel, I don't sleep. I just lie there, in her dark bedroom, and exist in the moment I never, ever want to end.

I WAKE up the next morning to a call. My phone is deep in the pockets of my jeans, the ringer going off like something's on fire. Incessant and irritating.

Birdie is naked beside me, one of her thighs tucked between mine. We're in the most complicated position I can remember ever actually sleeping in, and I curse at the damn phone, figuring it'll stop before it wakes up Birdie, but whoever's calling has an urgent need to fuck up my Sunday morning or a total disregard for getting their ear blasted with obscenities—probably both, because whoever it is doesn't leave a voice mail, but they do call back.

"Motherfuck…" I whisper against Birdie's hair and climb over her. I lean over the side of the bed, refusing to drag myself away from her long, naked limbs, and grab my jeans. The phone is blowing up in the pocket when I finally answer it with a bark.

"What?" I demand, not giving a shit who it is.

"Yo, man, it's me. We got to roll."

I hold the phone away and check the time. "Arrow, it's not even eight on a fucking Sunday. What the fuck, man?"

"The client I want help with is on the move today. I got a message from the wife that her husband was up early. I'm at the car rental place now, setting up an account for you. How soon can you be here?"

I groan and look back at Birdie. She's rubbing her face and rolling over in bed. The last thing I want to do is leave this. Leave her. Mia is probably going to be with Alice and Morris until, at the earliest, late morning… I mean, kids at sleepovers usually stay up late and wake up late, right? If I stay, Birdie and I can repeat last night once, twice, who knows how many times before we need to be anywhere.

"Crow? Man, you got a ride here?"

I sigh. While I don't relish the idea of ending what was the most amazing night of the last decade—fuck, maybe of my life—if I want more nights like that, I need to provide. I need to take steps to be the man I want to be in every way, not just a fuck machine who thinks with his dick. As easy as doing exactly that could be with Birdie, her sleep-mussed hair barely covering her breasts.

"Give me a half hour," I tell him. "I'll figure it out."

I lean over and kiss Birdie's hair. "Baby… Birdie," I tease, stroking the strands away from her face.

She opens her eyes, and when she grins, my dick throbs and my body forgets all about Arrow and any job he might have.

"Good morning, gorgeous," she mumbles. She reaches for me. "Coming back to bed?"

I hang my head and sigh. "Arrow's got a client on the move. He wants me to work today."

She looks disappointed for a moment. "Noooo," she mumbles. "Nooooo." She sits up in bed, clutching the sheets to her chest. "Is this because you think I'll give you food poisoning if I try to make breakfast? I promise, I've got more frozen sausage and egg biscuits downstairs."

She's grinning, her gray eyes as light as the sky after a rain. Something's different between us now, and it's not just the fact that we're both naked in her bed. It's like a little wall, that steel behind her eyes, has been knocked back. I feel it too, lighter. Safer. Like I can trust this. I can trust her.

"You're nuts," I say, claiming her lips with mine. "Last night was fucking perfect. You're perfect. Whatever you feed me for breakfast…" I shake my head. "All right, we'll cook together. When we have time. Another morning." It's a reach, a leap, but I need to believe this wasn't a one-and-done. I need to believe she'll want this again as much as I already know I do.

I lift her chin with my fingertips. "I'm sorry," I tell her. "I wish I could spend the whole day naked with you. I'd stay for as long as you'd have my ass."

"Mmm-hmm, that ass," she sighs. She sits up

straight and takes my hand in hers. "You should go," she says. "If you want to give this PI thing a try." She lifts the back of my hand to her lips and kisses my sparrow. "By the time you come back, I'll have condoms."

I growl and lunge at her, kissing her lips and fisting her hair. God, even first thing in the morning, she's sexy as fuck. She meets my kiss again and again, until finally, she's the one to pull away.

"Unless you want to spend the entire day like this… which, I'd be damn happy to do…let's get you on the road. You want me to drop you off?"

I nod. "That would be great. You mind if I shower? Since I'm putting the same clothes on I wore yesterday, at least Arrow won't have to smell all this on me."

She laughs and climbs out of bed. She strides naked to the hall closet and pulls out towels, a fresh bar of soap, and a brand-new toothbrush.

"Help yourself," she says. "I'll go start coffee."

I shower quickly, stepping around Mia's colorful bath toys and bath products that look more like paints than soaps or shampoos. I'm surprised at how many things a kid her age needs just to shower, but it's not a bad thing. After spending years showering in flip-flops with a stale sliver of soap to my name, all the products and choices feel like humanizing luxuries. I'm glad they have them, and if I can contribute to giving Mia and Birdie that kind of financial stability, I'll do the work, take the job. Swallow my hesitation and give this thing a real chance.

Not just for me. For Mia. For Birdie. And the future I am starting to hope the three of us can have together.

I leave my wet towel hanging over the bar that holds a palm-tree-printed shower curtain and put on my clothes from last night. The smell of coffee greets me, and when I head downstairs, Birdie is dressed in a long sleep shirt, but she's wearing nothing underneath.

"Seriously..." I groan and take the travel mug of coffee from her. "If you want to distract me from going anywhere today..." I slide a hand up the back of her shirt and fondle her firm, smooth ass.

She leans her head against my chest. "That wasn't the plan, but..." She lifts her face to mine and says, "Two minutes. I need pants and a bra. Be right back."

She's gone for closer to ten minutes, so I text Arrow that I'm just getting a ride and will be on the way any minute. We head out when Birdie comes back down, her hair in a messy bun on the top of her head. She's got on skintight yoga pants and a tank top instead of the loose sleep shirt. Just remembering what's underneath that tiny bit of fabric, the tasty berries of her nipples, makes me want to forget all about Arrow and any shitty job.

But Birdie slips on sunglasses, and we head out to the car. "First time I've driven since this all started," she says, climbing behind the wheel.

I reach across from the passenger side and hold her hand. "Too soon? How are you feeling?"

"I'm great," she says confidently. "I really am. I'm going to be okay."

We drive in silence for two miles to the car rental place, lacing and unlacing our fingers. It's a peaceful silence, like we're both still stuck in the erotic haze of her bedroom and not being forced out into the real world. I'm okay making that feeling last as long as possible. When we pull in, I turn to face her. "Be safe today. Take it easy. If you need anything at all, you need me to pick up Mia, anything, you call. Got it?"

She leans over, and we kiss, a long, sweet taste of tongues, the faint flavor of coffee on our mingled breath.

"Have a good day at work, sweetie," she teases. "I'll be fine. But I'll keep in touch."

I finish the coffee and leave the travel mug with her. Then I get out of the car and close the door. Before she pulls away, we spend a solid thirty seconds staring at each other through the closed window.

"Much as I love young love—" a voice comes from behind me just as I feel a hand clap on to my shoulder "—work's a-awaiting."

Birdie waves at Arrow and blows me a kiss good-bye. Then she pulls away.

"That seemed cozy," Arrow says.

I don't know the guy well, and while Leo vouched for him, I still don't know Leo that well yet. I just grunt and get down to business. "So, what's the job?"

Arrow points at Birdie. "Hey, man, I didn't mean to pry. I'm happy for you. After all you've been through, if you're picking up the pieces in your private life, that's cool. I meant no disrespect."

I roll my shoulders and nod. "Thanks, man. All good. What's the gig here?"

As much as I'm sure Arrow's trying to be cool with me, we're not friends. Might never be. If I work for him, I need to maintain that distance and detachment. I'm still not all that excited about following cheaters or scammers, so dragging me out of bed with the promise of work is all that I am up for right now. Braiding hair with my new best friend Arrow isn't in the playbook.

"Yeah, all right. Let's head in."

We go inside the rental office where Arrow has set me up as an authorized renter on his corporate account.

"Obviously, this isn't for personal use if you're not on a job," he tells me. "But if you're working a case, I want you in a rental."

"Got it." I hand over my license and insurance info to the guy behind the desk, a squeaky-clean-looking college kid in a golf shirt embroidered with the logo of the rental place.

"Good morning, Mr. Taylor." The kid looks at my

license and says my name, all professional and serious. His close-cut blond hair and deep tan remind me a little too much of the kids I intervened on behalf of that night so long ago, and a shiver runs up my spine. Is this a subtle sign that I shouldn't be here? Shouldn't be doing this? Or am I looking for signs because I'd rather be eating Birdie for breakfast than chasing cheaters on a Sunday morning?

I look away from the kid with his innocent eyes and peach-fuzz face and get down to the job. Arrow's got a slim folder in his hands. While the kid runs my identification through the system, Arrow explains.

"We go at this old-school," he says. "I'd prefer you not have any client images or data on your personal devices." He hands me a cell phone—it's a nice one. Newer than the one I have. "Use this for all client work. Even for mapping or Googling and other basic functions. That way, if the phone is ever confiscated or recovered, it'll be traceable to me, the licensed agent."

"Wait...there's a license involved?" This is news to me.

"Yeah," Arrow explains. "If you want to testify at trials or work with insurance companies and lawyers, you've got to be legit. There's a background check, education, and private investigator licensing requirements. But I'm only going to send you on what I call the civilian cases. You can follow cheating spouses and basic crap that won't ever make it to court."

I'm sure Arrow thinks what he's saying is going to bring me some comfort, but it does the opposite. If there's a background check involved and state licensing requirements, I'm damn sure I won't pass. Felony convictions don't bar me from every type of job, but I'm going to guess if PIs are regulated by the state of Florida, they won't be too keen on me spying on private citizens with my background.

"You know I have a record, man." I don't want to press the issue because I'm damn sure there's no way Arrow *doesn't* know. But I want to make sure.

He nods. "That's why I want you on board. You can talk the talk with people I never could. Consider this a paid internship. I'm trying you out, and you're trying this out. If you like it and do a good job, I'll cover the costs of getting you legal with the state to be licensed."

That all sounds well and good in theory, but what's he going to do if I get pulled over in a rented car with a phone that doesn't belong to me because I'm tailing somebody who notices me? Calls the cops because a strange man is following him or her?

I scrub my face with my hand, not sure this is where I want to be or what I want to be doing at all.

"Here." Arrow hands me the folder. "I'll pay you in cash for today just in case this doesn't work out. Inside is five hundred. Use the money to fill the tank on the rental before you return it. That's all yours, minus the gas."

I take the manila folder and open it. Inside is a printout with some factual information about the guy I'll be tailing. His picture, a picture of his car with the license plate up close. Arrow points to a small map. "That's his home address. His wife texted this morning that he said he was going to play golf at the Falcon Ridge Country Club. 10:20 a.m. tee time." He checks his watch. "You've got over an hour. I'd head to the house and watch him leave. Follow him to the club and confirm that's where he goes."

I have a million questions spinning through my head.

It's one day of work. If it goes well, I'll hold Arrow to his promise to get me set up and legit with the state as a PI. And if it doesn't, I made a bit of cash and can put the whole experience behind me.

Arrow's giving me a list of instructions, explaining what documents I'll need, what photos I'll need to take, and how to do it subtly and without calling too much attention to myself. It feels like a lot of trickery and deception and dishonesty. But this is a legit profession. Arrow is licensed, and if he's willing to vouch for me and back all this shit up... It's an honest day's work, even if it doesn't feel so honest.

I grab the keys to the rental car and memorize the code to the phone Arrow gave me. As I walk out into the lot to grab my totally nondescript rental sedan, I look back into the rental office. And I just hope that the preppy behind the counter isn't some kind of sign.

A warning.

14

BRIDGET

I'M SMILING, THINKING ABOUT LAST NIGHT, FEELING light as air, when there's a knock at my door. I haven't even showered yet, so the smells of Crow and the fun we had last night still cling to my skin and hair.

I check the peephole and see an elderly man I don't recognize. I open the door a crack.

"Good morning," I say to him. "Can I help you?"

"Hello, ah…"

The sun is bright, and the man is blinking like he can't quite see me through the glare.

"I…I was wondering…" The man was once tall, but his stooped shoulders and sunken cheeks show his age. He's well-dressed in nicely pressed khakis and a short-sleeved dress shirt, but he looks confused and disoriented. I don't recognize him as one of my neighbors, so

I'm immediately concerned he's in some kind of distress. I look up and down the street for an unfamiliar car or other people, but my street looks exactly the same as it always does. Nothing unusual except the man on my doorstep.

"Sir," I ask, "are you okay? Do you know where you are?"

"I do, yes…" He's staring at me, looking lost and like the polar opposite of knowing where he is. "Is your…mother here?"

"Let me grab my phone." I shut the door behind me and grab my cell phone. Old man or not, I'm not going to invite a stranger into my home, but I'll happily go outside with my phone and see if I can be of help. Before I head back out, I check the peephole again. The man's still standing there, looking down at his shoes. Not moving. So, I grab my keys and open the door, then join him on the patio.

When I open the door, the man says, "I know she's gone. I guess when I got here, my mind just went back, and I… It was habit or hopeful thinking. I don't know. I'm sorry."

I narrow my eyes at him. "Who are you?" I ask. "Did you know my mother?"

His eyes are the same rainy gray that mine are. "I sure did. And I know you too, Birdie."

I cross my arms over my chest as a small flare of alarm courses through my body. "Who the hell are you?" I demand. "What do you want?"

Old or not, this man is a stranger to me. And he's scaring me.

"I'm your father, Birdie. I'm sorry to surprise you this way. I know it's been a long time."

When he says those words, it's like a thousand-pound weight falls on my chest. I suck in a lungful of air and glare at him.

"I don't believe you. What's your name?" I demand.

"James Sanderson," he says quietly. "Your mom called me Jimmy. I should have extended my condolences a long time ago. I know it's been a very long time, but I thought maybe we could talk."

In that moment, the world beneath my feet feels like it's shifting. I'm hot, I'm cold, I'm shaking, and I'm furious.

"Your condolences?" I blurt. "You're here to extend your condolences? Mom's been gone for months. And you—you've been out of my life for twenty-five years, *Jimmy*." I say his name like it tastes bad in my mouth. Because it does. "No," I say. "You cannot do this. You can't just show up on my doorstep now. No."

I look the man over, in shock and disbelief that this is the man who created me. We look so alike, it's impossible to deny the relation. I always thought I looked like my mother, not that it matters all that much. But I suppose since I didn't have many memories of my dad, not having a photo to look at to know where I came from, I searched all the harder for a resemblance to Mom. But looking at this man now, even in his advanced age, I see it. The same steely eyes. The same nose... I mean, it's almost as if someone took his nose and put it right on my face. My lips are fuller, so those I'm sure I got from Mom. No matter how his presence makes me feel, there's no denying this man is my father.

"You're not welcome here," I say, a crushing wave of anger and sadness rushing over me. "Don't you ever come back." I think of Mia, of how she would feel if she were here and this man showed up on my doorstep. "I mean it. Stay away from me, and stay the hell away from my daughter."

He doesn't say anything, just looks at his shoes as I go inside, and I slam the door behind me and turn the dead bolt.

Fury and sadness wash over me, and I can't decide what to do first. I want to scream and throw something. But part of me wants to run after him. Demand answers. Hurl insults at him for every day he missed, every moment Mom and I struggled because of his deception and lies.

I throw myself onto the couch and start crying. The tears flow, hot and furious. I'm gasping for air and beating the couch cushion to vent some of my emotions. It's all too much. The pleasure of last night. The pain of this morning. I feel like I'm going to lose my mind if I don't release some of these emotions, and I think if Jimmy is still there, I'm going to take all of this out on him. He wants to talk—screw talking. I'll scream in his face and make him see what he's done, how many lives he's hurt being a piece-of-shit, lying deadbeat.

In a rush, I get up and yank the door open. I half hope he's still there. If he is, I'll demand answers. I'll let him in if only so I can get what I want for once. But of course, when I look out the door, he's gone.

My disappointment that he's gone starts to take over my anger.

It's not fair that I should be in this position. That I should feel like a bad person for not letting him just walk into my house and invite himself over for a catch-up. That I should feel this mix of guilt and shame because I'm so mad and I want to take it out on him. It's not fair he left us. Not fair he lied.

I pace my house frantically, wondering what he could have wanted after all this time. The usual maybe. He's sick or feeling guilty or something bad happened, and he wanted me to know about it. I don't know. Can't even guess. If he's dying and wanted to say goodbye and make peace…

No. No. No. No.

I take a few deep breaths and try to calm myself down. I'm feeling dizzy and stressed and my head is throbbing, but it's just a warning. It's not a full headache yet, but I realize I'm crying so hard that I'm probably dehydrating myself. I stumble into the kitchen and grab a glass of water and a fist full of tissues from the powder room. I take some pain meds for my head and drink a whole glass of cold water, the liquid cooling my overheated mouth and throat.

I pull out an old picture of myself lying facedown on a soft baby blanket, a blanket I still have in a closet upstairs. I'm playing with a toy and smiling, the tiny tips of two brand-new teeth poking through my baby gums. That sweet little child had no idea what life had in store for her. I trace my fingertips along my baby face and head, and the tears come. No one else is going to cry for me. No one else cares. I've always been alone, abandoned by unreliable men, and so has my mother. No matter what James Sanderson wants, I don't want him.

I SPEND a good amount of time in the bathtub, reading and thinking. It's impossible not to feel pissed off that I had the most amazing night with Crow, his body, his words, our essence so caring and powerful together, and the very next morning, James Sanderson shows up. Two men who appeared in my life at the exact worst times.

After who knows how long in the bath, I get a text from Alice offering to drop Mia off. I accept the help, because honestly, I'm in no condition to drive or to leave the bathtub until the last possible second.

As I'm toweling my hair dry, thankful that the headache that seemed about to start is keeping its distance, there's a knock at the door.

I head downstairs, hair still wet but in comfy sweats and a loose T-shirt. My heart flips, and my body responds immediately when I open the door.

"Hi," I say, trying to ignore the tingle of my core and the way my breasts ache with the memory of his stubble scraping so deliciously against my sensitive skin. My body may have a mind of its own, but my face can't hide where my head is.

Crow's face falls when he sees me. "Hey." He lifts my chin with his fingers. "What happened? You look like you've been crying."

I step out of his hold. "I'm...I'm fine. Mia's on her way back, so I don't think I should talk about it."

Crow snaps his lips together but makes no attempt to follow me. "Birdie," he says. "What the hell happened? If this is about us… If you've having second thoughts about what happened…"

I shake my head sadly. "No, it's just…complicated. I really don't have time to talk about it right now. I'm sorry."

I don't even know where to begin. Part of me wants to run into his arms and pound against his chest, release all the sadness and rage inside, but Mia's on her way home. I'm fighting a headache. And I don't even know how I feel. Guilt. Sadness. It's a roller coaster, and right now, I just want to get off the ride.

I'm so lost in my own confusion, I don't ask about Crow's day. I don't ask if he's okay. I'm just focused on keeping it together for myself and for Mia. That's how it has to be.

"Don't have time," Crow echoes. He takes two steps back from me, his face withdrawn, shuttered from any emotion. "I understand. I'd better get back to the compound anyway." He walks up to me and looks like he wants to hug me, hold me, but I can't even look at him. If I do, my carefully constructed walls will come crumbling down. When the floodgates open, pain—real pain—will consume me, and right now, I can't give in to that. My dad doesn't deserve that. I'm not going to let him steal the small shred of peace I have left.

"I'll text you later," I say, trying to muster a smile for Crow. But I can't. Can't look at his gorgeous face, so complicated and caring.

An SUV eases to the curb in front of my house, and Alice, Zoey, and Mia climb out. Mia runs for me, happy and babbling.

"Mama, we had the best time ever. I didn't want to come home because we have so much more to do, but then we got exciting news. You won't even believe it."

I hug my daughter and try to shove aside the emotions and stress of the day. "Hi, baby. I'm so glad you had fun." I look at Alice. "Thank you," I tell her. I truly mean it. I am so, so grateful that Mia wasn't here when James—my dad—showed up. I can't even let my mind go back to last night, but Alice is looking from Crow to me, and her face looks a bit troubled.

"Did you guys have a good evening?" she asks gently.

Crow grunts and bends down to look at some artwork that Mia's brought. She and Zoey are excitedly explaining the pictures.

"We did," I say but then quickly change the subject. "What's this exciting news?"

Alice claps her hands together. "Well, all the excitement of the shower yesterday must have made that baby eager to arrive. Lia went into labor in the middle of the night."

She pulls out her cell phone to show us a picture of Lia in a surgical suite. "Her due date is still five weeks away, but the little guy was not to be stopped. Lia had an emergency C-section at about five this morning. Mama and baby are doing great."

I look over at the images on her phone, the wrinkly little red-faced boy in Leo's arms and Lia, her hair trapped under a surgical cap, her body draped and covered up.

Zoey and Mia have already seen the pictures, but they drop what they're doing to coo over the little guy again.

"Mama, isn't he so cute? I can't wait to be old enough to babysit." Mia sounds so happy, I feel my own sadness even more acutely.

Even though I just met them yesterday, I'm happy for Leo and Lia. They're a sweet little family unit, and that's exactly as it should be. Just hours ago, I was looking at my own baby pictures, and this is another small kick to my already tender heart.

"Did they name him?" I ask.

Alice shakes her head. "Lia wants to try out a few names and see how they feel before they commit." She laughs, but it's a loving sound. "That's so Lia. I wouldn't be surprised if the boy goes through ten names before they choose Moonstone or something."

She holds out her phone to show Crow the pictures,

and I see the way his face softens. It's as if the protective shield he put up when he got here is melting away. He smiles but doesn't say anything.

"That leads me to a small problem," Alice continues. "Lia didn't have time to make arrangements for her business before the baby came. She was planning to hire a temp to run the doggie day care center part time, but she won't be able to come in and chase after dogs now that she's had a C-section. I have an office just two stores down in the strip mall where Lia runs the day care. I can help you get acclimated, and as long as you're not afraid of dogs, I thought maybe you'd be open to helping with the Canine Crashpad for a few weeks, maybe longer…"

She's looking at me expectantly, and it registers that she's offering me the one thing I need right now. A job.

"Me?" I ask and look at Crow.

"We're going to need you too," she says, tapping Crow on the shoulder. "With the C-section, Leo's likely going to want to take as much time off as the shop can manage. If you're available, Crow, I think Tim's going to need you closer to full time if you can fit it in around your other projects."

He nods. "Whatever he needs," he says.

I wonder how Crow feels about that, working in the auto shop instead of his construction plans. And he worked today with Arrow, so I wonder where that leaves everything.

Alice is talking about how much they can pay me, and she explains it won't have benefits, but Lia was planning on taking at least two to three months off when the baby was born, so if I'm game to give this a try, she's sure we can talk about anything I need as the weeks go on.

"I can meet you at the day care in the morning," she says, "if you're available."

I appreciate what she doesn't say, but which I think is implied. If I feel well enough.

"Mama." Mia looks like someone has just given her a winning lotto ticket. "Are you going to do it? You're going to work with puppies?"

I look at Alice and consider the opportunity. My brain is swimming with the developments of the day, and my heart is troubled. But a job—a paying job—with someone who won't look badly on my termination, who won't bother checking references because they already know what they need to know about me… I'd be a fool to pass it up.

"I'd love to," I say.

Mia and Zoey are high-fiving, and Zoey is explaining everything she knows about dogs, while Crow is standing there looking off… Glum.

Alice texts me the address of the building and tells

me when to meet her in the morning. Then she gathers up Zoey and gives us all hugs goodbye.

"Thank you," she says to me. "Lia's worked so hard to build this business, and I can help a little here and there, but I've got my hands full with the office and..." She grins, and I know she means her own little bean.

"Of course," I say. "Thank you. This will be great. Really great."

The more I think about it, the more I feel good about it. I'll have a job and a chance to build up great work experience so that Alice and Lia can give me references when she's ready to come back to work. I can put the termination behind me, and while I won't have benefits right away, I can work on figuring out doctors and insurance issues, knowing that I at least will have some income coming in.

"Crow," Alice says, "you need a ride back?"

He looks at me, his expression dark and unreadable. "I've got to return this rental," he says. "You'll be driving Mia to school in the morning?" he asks.

I know what he's implying. If we're both starting new jobs tomorrow—well, mine will be new, but his will be more hours at the place he's worked part time— our little routine of him driving Mia to school and spending the day working here... All of that is over.

"Yeah," I say quietly. "I'll drive her."

Alice is watching our exchange with interest and a noticeable expression of concern.

"I was just heading out before you got here," Crow says to Alice. "Mind following me to the car rental place?"

"Not at all," she says. "Zoey, say bye to Mia."

While Mia and Zoey say goodbye, I stand by and just watch them. Two sweet, little things untarnished so far by too many of life's blows. I know in my heart that's not true. Crow told me that Alice had a manipulative ex. And Mia knows disappointment better than anyone, having the dad she's got. He's not much better than the man who showed up on my doorstep today, for that matter.

We're all just walking through life, bouncing between the heartaches we cause and the ones we carry. I'm overwhelmed and tired by it all, and I just want a few minutes of normal life. My daughter and me. No more strangers, no more surprises. No matter how wonderful most of the people and surprises have been.

Alice and Zoey head for the door, and I thank her again for hosting Mia. "Next time, we'll have Zoey here," I promise.

Alice nods and tells me she'll see me in the morning. Crow says goodbye to Mia, who gives him a warm hug before bouncing upstairs. Then we're alone.

"Are you..." Crow starts but then changes his mind. "Can I text you later?" he asks.

"Of course." I want to say more, to explain what happened today, but Alice is waiting, and I'm so worn-out, I just lean against the door and watch him walk to the rental car. He gets in and drives off without even waving goodbye.

15

CROW

"Yo, hear the news?" Morris is in the kitchen of the compound, pouring himself a glass of water. "Tiny's a fucking grandpa."

"Heard all about it. Your old lady filled me in and showed me pics." Alice is outside waiting for Morris, so I clap him on the shoulder. "She's outside waiting for you with Zoey."

Morris drains the water in a couple of sips and slaps the counter. "Can't keep the ladies waiting." He walks past and then stops. "See you at the shop in the morning? You gonna be able to fill in for Leo?"

Even if I didn't want to fill in for Leo, if a club brother has a need, every one of us will do whatever it takes to be there.

I nod. "First thing."

Morris rubs his hands together. "Construction plans

are just on hold. We'll get back to it, if that's what you still want. How's Birdie's reno going?"

I nod again. "Almost done."

Morris cocks his chin. "Something up? You two looked pretty damn smitten yesterday. Something you want to talk about?"

I shake my head, not even sure where to start, what to say. "Thanks, man." I clap him on the shoulder. "You got a wife and kid waiting. Go on. We'll catch up another time."

Morris claps me back but then meets my eyes. "Heartaches are like headaches," he says. "When they come on strong, they take up all the air in the room. Make it hard to see a time when things will feel normal again. But shit always passes," he reminds me. "Sometimes you just need a little time and patience."

I flick him in the gut. "You practicing dad-speak on me, man?"

He's grinning under his beard. "Go fuck yourself, smartass," he shouts, and he heads out to meet Alice and Zoey.

I grab a beer from the fridge and walk into my room. I lie back on the bed and check my phone. Nothing. No missed calls, no unread texts. Well, that's not entirely true. I have three voice mails from that New York number that I assume is my dad. I just haven't had it in me to listen. And I still don't.

After spending an amazing night with Birdie, I don't know what I expected. More? I mean, fuck, of course I want more. After just one taste, I'll never get my fill of that woman. Her sighs, her cries, the way she shuddered and licked me... Fuck. My dick twitches just remembering last night. But even more than my body, it's my heart that's on the line now.

I think about how cool she was this afternoon, and it shatters me—something I didn't think anyone could do anymore.

Maybe things are moving too fast. Maybe she's having second thoughts. I don't think I disappointed her last night, but who knows? I don't want to assume the worst, but it's hard not to contemplate that she's decided an ex-con isn't the best bet for her right now. Our chemistry is off the fucking charts. I get along with her kid. I don't even mind her cooking that reminds me more of prison than I care to admit. If that doesn't add up to a future, I don't think I'll ever know what one feels like.

I consider texting her, asking if she's all right, but fuck. It all feels like me chasing her. This is the part of women I haven't had to deal with in so long. I'm as out of practice at understanding them as I am at fucking them. Does Bridget need space? Does she want me to reach out? I don't know, and I'm damned sure whatever I do will be the wrong thing.

That's just how this day has gone. I ended up giving

Arrow the money back and leaving the gig. Once I saw the old man I was supposed to be tailing coming out of the country club with his arm around a young blonde who was definitely not the same woman as the wife who'd hired Arrow, I just felt sick.

When I thought about climbing between cars and taking pictures—giving this woman the proof she wanted to back up her suspicions that her man was cheating... It all just felt cheap and dirty and wrong. Taking money when I'm not licensed but should be... The whole thing made my stomach flip and a feeling of intense dread come over me.

I ended up texting Arrow from my personal phone and telling him I couldn't do it. He was out on another job, so he just said, *Got it*, but I could tell he was pissed.

Fuck.

I punch my pillow and roll onto my side, wishing like hell I had a road map for what to do. Work. Relationships. Friends. This entire reentry into real life would be impossible without this club. I can't imagine where I'd be if I didn't have this place to live, friends who don't hassle me for rent, and a bunch of guys looking out for me, trying to find me work. If I look at it that way, on some level, I can respect what Arrow's trying to do, even if I don't agree with it or like it.

Since I'm feeling shitty about just about everything, I decide to listen to my voice mails. I can't feel much worse, so I might as well get everything out of the way.

As I expect, all three calls are from my dad. What I don't expect is how he sounds.

"Son?" I hear Dad's voice, but goddamn, he sounds older. More frail. "Son, I heard you've been released, and I just… I just… Call me."

The second message sounds even more tense. I can't tell if Dad's angry, pissed off, or some combination of both. "Logan? It's your father. Call me, son. I want to hear your voice."

And then the last one. "Logan, it's…your dad. I… Ah, never mind…" His voice cracks at the end and gets farther away, as if he's talking to himself and not to me. Something inside me cracks open hearing the defeat and the distance in the message. This time, he does not say call me. He just hangs up the phone.

I grab my pillow and toss it at the wall, desperate to vent some of my pent-up emotions. My father hasn't once offered me a place to live. Always welcome in his home? He loves me? That's not the kind of relationship we've ever had. I don't know what he expects from a call. A pleasant catch-up? Stories of the murderers and the con artists and other scumbags I did my best to steer clear of so I could stay out of trouble and alive for the last seven years?

Did he think I'd just pack up my nonexistent clothes

and nonexistent money and jump in my nonexistent car and drive across the country for a reunion dinner? I strip off all my clothes and change into shorts. Tiny's at the hospital playing granddad. Morris is home with his family. And me? I've got a couple of sad-sounding voice mails and a heart made of stone.

I lace up my running shoes and leave my phone behind. I don't need anyone. I don't want anything. I just want it all to be a little easier. And it's never going to be. So, I walk out the compound door and start running.

THE NEXT MORNING, I get up early and text Tim. He's already at the shop, but he wants to go visit his new nephew, so he confirms I should come by as soon as I can to cover him for the day. I can't stop thinking about Birdie. About our night together. About whatever happened to shut things down between us just as fast as they started to open.

It's early enough that she's probably already dropped Mia off at school, so I type out a simple text but then delete it. I toss the phone onto my bed and get dressed, but I'm in agony trying to decide whether I should reach out to Birdie or not. I'm like a fucking teenager. Gaga over a girl and consumed with indecision about what to do.

If she's working at Lia's Canine Crashpad and I'm over at Leo and Tim's shop, I'm going to see her. I might as well break the seal and take the pain if that's what's coming. It'll make things a lot less awkward later.

Logan: *Good morning, gorgeous. Just wanted to wish you a good day.*

I'm reading the text over for the thousandth time when Morris knocks loudly on my open door.

"Hey, asshole, I hear you got a job to get to." He's got mirrored sunglasses over his eyes, and he's dangling something in his hand. "For you."

I grab the set of keys from his hand. "What's all this?"

"Leo wanted me to give you one of the master keys for the shop so you can come and go as you need to," he says. "That's the silver key."

"And this?" I know by the logo on the black plastic fob exactly what it is, but I have to press him. "Come on, man. What are you doing?"

Morris just nods. "Crow, you need a vehicle and not just your bike or those peg legs."

"I can't…"

Morris slides his glasses onto his forehead and looks me over. "Can I be real with you?"

I chuckle. "What would you say if I said no?"

"Fuck off," he says. "Listen, man. I know better than anybody how long and hard the road is to making something for yourself. Look all around you. Tiny's just now figuring out how to be in a family after being cut off from his daughter for years. I found Alice long past the age when an asshole like myself should have hoped for a family, for something real. And now look at me."

"You ready for all that?" I ask. "Diaper duty, man. Never thought I'd see the day."

"That's my point." Morris is looking me in the eye, now, man-to-man, brother-to-brother. "I never thought I'd see the day that you'd be back here. When you went away…" He scrubs a hand over his face. "You were missed, man. You were missed. A brother, a friend. You belong here. But you're going to have to accept that being part of this brotherhood isn't just about riding and bitches and getting wasted. Not anymore. A lot changed while you were away, and I think it's for the better."

I'm not sure where this little pep talk is going, but I shake my head. "You sure got fucking soft."

Morris throws a punch that intentionally doesn't land in my gut. "Some things haven't changed. I could still beat your ass, Crow." He levels his gaze at me. "I want you to use my truck until you've got one of your own. We're brothers. We help each other out. No questions asked, no debt. We don't fucking keep score. Now, go to work."

I try to refuse, try again to hand him back the keys, but Morris puts a hand on my shoulder and squeezes.

"Shut your mouth and listen." His words are stern but sincere. "Most people don't get a second chance in life. Don't waste a moment of yours thinking you're not good enough for Birdie. You are. You hear me? You are. You want her, don't let fear or pride or anything else get in the way. Now, go to work, asshole."

I clutch the keys in my fist and watch Morris walk out of my room. With a renewed sense of purpose in my chest, I grab my phone. I delete the lame-ass text I had composed to Birdie and type up a new one.

Good morning, gorgeous. I can't stop thinking about you. I'll see you at work. Talk soon.

I don't ask permission, and I'm not going to apologize. I want Birdie. And Morris is right. If she's my second chance, I'm not going to let her slip away. Not for anything. I hit send, grab my shit, and rummage in my closet for my old leather vest. It's been here, way in the back, since the week I surrendered myself. I haven't put it on since, but today, I'm going to be me again. I slide my arms through the sleeves and adjust the fit. I've lost a bit of weight since I wore this last, but only the extra I needed to lose. My arms look more cut than they ever did, and I look like someone I remember. Someone I haven't seen in a long fucking time. I look like me.

And I feel good.

WHEN I PULL into the parking lot of the strip mall, the entire place is quiet. Tim's truck is in the back lot, and I see both Alice's and Birdie's cars. I park the truck and walk up to the Canine Crashpad first. I can see through the plate glass that Birdie is inside, her head down and her back to the glass.

I yank open the doors, ready to face whatever she's feeling. If she doesn't want me, if she regrets what we did, I'm gonna take it like a man. Stake my claim, say my piece, but then I'll accept her feelings and move on. I need to do this. Need to do something that makes me feel like, whatever the consequences, I'm making a move again. I'm taking back the shame, the fear, and putting myself out there.

"Birdie?"

I'm stunned to see her shoulders are shaking, her face wet with tears. There are a half dozen dogs running around and playing with one another, and when I open the door, the barking starts.

Shit. This cannot be good for her head.

"Shh, shh. All right, all right." I bend down to let the

pups lick and sniff me, and within a couple minutes, they are all relaxed and back to running after one another or snoozing on beds. I immediately turn my attention to Bridget.

"This is no good," I tell her, shaking my head. "The barking, the noise…"

She doesn't say anything, but she launches herself into my chest. "Crow," she whispers.

I wrap my arms around her and breathe in her scent, the berries and vanilla of her hair bringing me back to the more intimate moments we spent in her bed. My body responds, but I need something else right now. I need to know exactly what's making my girl cry.

My girl.

It feels good to think it. Even better to say it.

"What happened?" I ask, lifting her chin so our eyes meet. "Baby, what's got my girl so wrecked?"

A tiny smile tips her lips even through the tears.

"Is it the noise? The dogs? Because—"

She shakes her head. "God, no. Lia's got some really good clients here. The dogs get excited when someone comes in, but the last hour I've been alone with them has been so easy, Crow. I can't believe this is a job. I've never had more fun. In fact, Alice is going to cover for me this afternoon so I can pick up Mia from school and bring her here. Lia keeps full records on every dog. Since Zoey's here so much, Lia only takes dogs who can be around children. Mia is going to lose her mind."

I stroke my thumb across Birdie's cheek, swiping away the hot tears. "So, what is it, then? Why the tears?"

"My head's a mess—not the headaches," she clarifies. "Something happened yesterday while you were working. I needed a minute to process it, and I didn't want Mia to know anything until I figured it out."

My chest tightens, and I start to feel my concern turn to anger. "What? Baby, I'm dying here. Who hurt you?"

She rests her forehead against my chest. "My father. Again."

I almost release a relieved breath because this is a battle I know. Shitty dads. "What'd he do? I thought you had no contact?"

She shakes a little in my arms. "He showed up at my front door," she says. "He wanted to talk."

"He fucking did what?" I'm starting to see red.

She shrugs. "I didn't let him say anything. I sent him away and told him to stay away."

"But it still hurts." I don't even have to ask. I know.

She nods. "I went from floating on a cloud after our...you know...and then—wham. The universe couldn't give me one morning to enjoy what I was feeling. James Sanderson had to show up out of nowhere. After all these years."

I listen as she talks about what happened, but I make a mental note of the man's name.

"What can I do?" I ask. "You want me to go talk to him?"

She rubs her face. "You would do that? You'd put yourself out to find out what he wants?"

I think about Arrow and realize we have ways of finding shit out about people. I just may not like doing it as a career. But if it helps me get something Birdie needs...

"I'd do anything for you," I admit. I hold her face in my hands. The morning sun is streaming through the plate glass of the Canine Crashpad, making Birdie's eyes look like silver stars. I kiss her forehead. "I know we haven't known each other long, and I'm not asking you for forever. Not yet. But you know I lost a lot of life from a stupid decision. I'm not going to make stupid decisions anymore. Not if I can help it. Letting you get away—that would be the stupidest mistake of my entire life."

She lifts up on her toes and crashes her mouth into mine. Our tongues tangle, and I grip her hips with my hands, pulling her tightly against me. Our bodies are pressed so close, I'm sure she can feel the bulge behind my zipper as it rises to meet her belly.

She runs her hands along my back and cups my ass, pulling us even closer. "Crow," she moans, "meeting you was luck. Keeping you is a choice. And I want this. I want you."

One of the little dogs is panting and whining at my ankle, which completely tears me out of the moment. But I think that's for the best.

"Unless you want me to take you right here," I grit out, "I'd better get to work."

She kisses my chin and cheeks and mouth again, her tongue flirting with my lower lip until I'm laughing and backing away.

"You're a bad influence…" I say.

"You just said I was a good decision," she teases. "Go to work." She releases me and nods. "Can you come over tonight? Mia will be home, but I'd really love to see you," she says. "Our first time might just have to be in my car on the way home."

"I'll be there, babe."

"Enough about me and my problems. How did yesterday go with Arrow?"

"It was only a one-time deal." I brush it off. Now's not the time for long stories. "That shit wasn't for me. I'd rather work in the shop or do construction."

She looks at me, a tilt to her chin like she knows there's got to be more to it, but she doesn't press. "There's a lot of ways to make a living," she says. She bends down and picks up a tiny little dog that has bows in its hair. "Sometimes the things we need show up when we're ready for them."

"And maybe when you're not," I say, pointing to a large mutt who's currently taking a leak against a wall.

"Oh shit." She sets the little dog down on the floor. "Duty calls." She blows me a kiss. "Have a good day, babe."

One side of my mouth curls in a smile, and I head out toward the shop to get started on the day with Tim. On my way to the far corner of the property, I pass the storefront office where Arrow works.

I tap the glass lightly, and when he sees me, he waves me in.

"Hey, man," I say. "You got a sec?"

Arrow motions for me to take a seat. "Plenty of seconds for you, man. What's up?"

I explain to Arrow that I'm sorry the gig isn't going to work out for me. We talk for a few about my worries, not wanting to work without a license when one could be required. How much I want to put my past behind me and not associate with people who scam for a living.

"Not you, man," I say, making sure my meaning is clear. "You know what I mean, though. If you'd spent the time I did with the people I did—"

Arrow holds up a hand. "Man, I get it. I honestly thought it could go either way. You'd either be really good at blending in with the clients or marks, or it wouldn't be a good fit. No skin off my nose either way, seriously."

"We cool, then?" I ask, extending a hand.

He claps mine in his and echoes, "We're cool."

I'm getting up to leave when I have a thought. "Would you be down for me hiring you for something? I just need a little information."

"You?" Arrow looks surprised. "What're you looking for? An old girlfriend or cellmate or something?"

I shake my head. "Name's James Sanderson. He's Birdie's father. She hasn't seen him in years, and he shows up at her door this weekend, wanting a family reunion."

"What're you looking for? Financials, tax records?"

"Shit, no, man. Just an address. Maybe a phone number. I want to know what he wants from Birdie."

He gives me a look. "She okay with you digging into her dad like that?"

I nod. "She asked me to."

"Well, shit, then." Arrow turns his monitor so it faces me. "You don't need me, then. Everything you're looking for is probably online. Look."

He punches in some searches using the man's name. We guess his approximate age, and he asks if I know anything else about him. Only two James Sandersons come up in the search. One is a kid, a twelve-year-old, who played in the Little League All-Star game, so we can rule that guy out.

The other one is a lawyer. There's an address for the law firm he runs.

"Forty partners," Arrow says, his eyes wide. "The dude makes bank. Founding partner of a firm this size?" He whistles through his teeth. "The guy may be a shit, but he's a rich shit."

Arrow sends a link to my phone with the address of the firm and a photo of James, Birdie's dad. "That's all you needed? That's nothing. No charge."

"Next time you feel like a cold one, it's on me," I tell him.

"I'll hold you to that," Arrow says.

As I head out, I'm not even surprised anymore that even Arrow, a guy who has nothing to gain from it, just Googled the information I needed. I could have done that myself, but I didn't even think about it. This is the new world I'm living in, though. I'll catch up. I'll figure shit out. But until then, it's humbling and pretty fucking amazing that I have more help and support around me than I could ever have imagined.

Now it's time to pay that shit forward.

16

BIRDIE

THE FIRST COUPLE OF WEEKS WORKING IN THE CANINE Crashpad have brought me everything I needed—some income, a place to focus my energy and time every day, and an excuse to be close to Crow. Alice opens the Crashpad for me and does all the early morning intake of the pups who stay the whole day. I come in by ten and take over, and then depending on what is going on, Alice and I take turns leaving the store and picking up both girls from their respective schools and bringing them back to the strip mall. Zoey and Mia play in the office or with me and the dogs until the shop closes at six.

As we've adjusted to the new routine, Crow and I have made a few adjustments of our own. Most days, Tim doesn't need Crow to open the shop but has him come in later and work until early evening, handling after-hours customer pickups and cleanup.

With a little creativity, I can drop Mia at school and make it back home by just after eight a.m. That means Crow can meet me back at the house, where we have one to two hours until one or both of us needs to be at work.

Which means we have a little time alone almost every day.

"Birdie…" The moment I close and lock the door, Crow's body is against mine, the heat of his chest pinning me back with delicious pressure.

I lean my head back against the door and close my eyes, Crow's lips and stubbly chin already rough against my mouth. His taste, the feel of his strong back beneath my hands—everything about Crow doesn't just feel good, he feels right.

I groan against his lips, opening my mouth to welcome him. "Baby," I sigh. "I'm happy to see you, but can we take this to the couch?"

He shocks me by picking me up in his arms and carrying me to the couch. I yank off my long-sleeved T-shirt and lean back against the cushions. He claims my nipples right through the thin fabric of my bra, my pulse quickening as his mouth awakens every nerve ending in my body.

I lean my head back and watch through my lashes as

he unfastens my bra and tosses it aside. His tongue works my right nipple until it is throbbing with pleasure that borders on pain. As he teases his scratchy beard against the reddened peak, I rub my thighs together, liquid heat gathering in my core. My breathing slows, and I weave my fingers through his hair, keeping his face close to my chest.

He feasts on my nipples, stroking and squeezing the fullness of each breast until I am breathless and wriggling with need.

"Crow," I rasp, my voice thick. "Today. Today's the day."

He immediately lifts his head and stares into my eyes. His lips are full and parted, his breath coming in long, aroused pants like mine. He doesn't say another word, just reaches out his hand and helps me off the couch.

We walk together up the stairs, holding hands. My being shirtless doesn't make it uncomfortable or awkward. We've been hoping for another date night to take things to the next level, but things just haven't worked out that way. I really didn't want our first time together to be while Mia was inches away in her room, but I also didn't want to rush in the morning after the school drop-off before heading out to work.

But I don't care about the "right" time anymore. I just want him. I want this man in every way. He's made my body reach heights with his fingers, his tongue, once even just by me grinding on his lap while he sucked my nipples. But today's the day. We have the protection situation sorted out, and we have at least an hour. I don't want to waste a minute more of it.

Once we're in my room, I wiggle out of my pants while Crow strips down to his boxer briefs.

"Wait," he says.

Before I climb into bed, we stand together, wearing just our underwear. He pulls me close to him and holds me there, my breasts flat against his bare chest and his hands on my lower back.

"Birdie," he says, "I'm so...happy. I never thought I'd feel this way again. Not just this—" he pats my ass with a sparrow-covered hand "—but this." He pulls back and meets my eyes. I can tell he's struggling with something.

He blinks hard, squinting a little, and releases me with one hand to tap at his chest.

"I didn't have the faith in myself to hope for anything even close to this. You're more than I could have asked for and everything I could dare to want. You're the answer to every dream I wouldn't allow myself to have."

I lean back so I can hold his face and watch his eyes as he tells me his truth. I want to see his face as I share mine.

"Crow," I whisper, my voice cracking a little. "Two imperfect halves make a pretty great whole."

He nods and grabs me roughly, kissing the top of my head and squeezing tight. I hold him too, marveling at the connection we're building. As much as I want what his heart has to offer, his body is doing things now that we're standing so close, and it's hard to ignore the enormous bulge pressing into my belly.

I work a hand between us and gently cup his balls through his briefs. He closes his eyes and sucks in air, but he quickly scoops me up and plants me on the bed. There's no gentle foreplay this time. He yanks my panties away from my hips, and before I can even lie back, his boxers are gone and he's centering himself between my legs.

"Birdie," he gasps, saying my name over and over.

He's rolled a condom over his length, and I can feel the tip of him gently nudging against my center. We're kissing, his teeth banging against mine as we tug at each other's hair and devour each other's mouths. The moment is frantic and needy, the lust we've let simmer and only partially satisfied over the past weeks now demanding everything we've held back.

I lift my knees high, spreading my thighs wide, and he taps my entrance only once before planting himself deep inside. He's holding his weight with his colorful, sculpted arms, every design and muscle working to support him as he bucks against my core. His pace is deep and slow, shallow and fast, but I can't keep track. I'm lost to the sensations, to the pleasure pounding its way along each nerve ending with his every thrust. I'm drenched for him, and he slides deep, the angles and ridges of his body perfectly fitting and forming to mine.

He moans and cries out my name, quickly withdrawing with fire in his eyes.

"Get on top," he demands, flopping onto his back.

I'm groggy with desire, my body shaky and my breath coming in small gasps. I center myself over his cock, my thighs wide over his hips. He inches toward the head of the bed, sitting with his back slightly supported by pillows.

"I want to watch you take me inside you."

I shift into a squatting position, my knees bent and legs open so I as lower myself onto his cock, he can look down between us and see every inch of his length disappear between my lips. He keeps one hand on my pussy, teasing the curls aside so he has an unobstructed view. My thighs quake and burn as I lower myself slowly, his mouth falling open as he watches. I can't look, can't see. My eyes are closed, and I'm supporting my weight as best I can, but it's so much. It's so good, the way I feel him stretch and stroke me.

I can't keep up this position any longer. My thighs

are trembling, and my pussy is pushing me to the point of no return.

"Crow," I gasp, dropping my knees to the bed and sinking fully onto his cock. I start to roll my hips, riding him hard and fast.

His hands are on my tits then, his fingertips teasing my nipples with tiny twists and tugs that send currents of fire through my body until, finally, I crash. The wave crests, and I'm riding high, calling out his name, my eyes closed and the most exquisite bliss pouring through my body in wave after wave after wave.

I'm sweating and trembling and near tears when he releases my nipples, and I open my eyes.

He helps me ease off his cock, and we lie with my back to his front, spooning together while I come down. He's kissing my hair and ears, his still-hard cock nudging my ass cheeks. He works the muscles of my backside with one hand, stroking and massaging until I feel one finger slide between my legs.

"Oh God," I moan. I'm satisfied and am starting to feel raw and full, but his finger between my lips is stroking my plentiful juices backward, wetting my tight pucker.

He lifts one of my thighs and holds it up while he slips back inside me. One thigh in the air and him deep inside me is all the pleasure I think I can take until I feel him shifting his weight a bit to make room for one hand to slide between us. He's thrusting slow and deep inside me, my moans and begging for him to go deeper unanswered until I feel the tiniest bit of extra pressure and realize the tip of his thumb is pressing against my pucker. When he fills me with just the tip of his finger, the pressure inside me goes white, and all sight and sound disappear into another wave of all-consuming fire.

I cry out and press my hips backward, my ass and pussy alive with his fullness. "Crow, oh my God…"

He comes way too soon, gritting my name and pounding his release in steady, rhythmic beats. He pulls his finger and his cock out but holds me firmly against him, our sweat and heat and tangled hair so intertwined I feel like we'll never separate. I take one quick peek at the clock and reassure myself we've got more time together. As my eyes flutter closed, I realize I never, ever want this feeling to end. I want this and him. Always.

CROW AND I SHOWER TOGETHER, which makes us dangerously close to being late for work, but I want to spend every second I can with him this morning. Even the moments I spend scrubbing away the sweat and smells of our passion.

I don't bother drying my hair and throw it up into a messy bun. While I'm grabbing clean clothes, Crow is on his phone. He's looking angrier and angrier, so I come around and grab him by the waist. He drops his head and jams his phone into his pocket. The warmth from our morning has faded fast, and he turns and plants a kiss on my head.

"Gotta run," he says, his voice tight. "See you at work?"

After what we just shared, I want him to tell me everything. Open up about the sudden shift in his mood. Whatever he's reading on his phone has to be what's caused this sudden change, but I don't know how to push him, whether to.

"Hey," I say gently, stroking the side of his face with a hand. "Are you okay?"

For a moment, he focuses his full attention on me. He leans down and sweeps a kiss across my lips. "Never better," he says, and I believe that he means it. But that doesn't mean there isn't a mask shielding me from what's going on behind his eyes. He holds me close and says again, "See you at work."

I head into the kitchen to get lunch and snacks ready to bring for both myself and Mia for after school, when there's a knock at the door. Crow just left, so I assume it's him and open the door to find another man at my door.

"Bridget." The elderly man nods. "I'm glad you opened the door."

I look the man over. from the steel-gray eyes that match mine to the stooped-over shoulders, all the way down to the pricey leather loafers on his feet.

"I told you I had no interest in this." I wave a hand at him. "I don't need to see you or speak to you. Now, if you don't mind…" I try to close the door, but he holds up a hand.

"Bridget, please," he says. "I only need a few minutes. And then I promise, I'll go."

He seems a lot less frail than he did the other day. The sun is shining on my face, and I pull my phone from the pocket of my jeans and check the time.

"I need to leave for work," I tell him. "This isn't a good time."

"I'm dying," he says, his voice low. "This may be the last chance I have to set things right."

I look him over closely, refusing to believe anything he says as truth. "Don't lie to me, James. Not now. Not like this."

There's something in his face that strikes me. It's raw and real, but it's not honesty. It's fear.

I debate stepping outside to talk to this stranger, to this man who somehow thinks he has a right to contact me, but he looks so pathetic, I decide to let him in.

I step back and wave at my couch, offering him a seat. "Ten minutes," I remind him, glaring.

He drops down onto my couch, staring at the pictures of my mom and Mia scattered throughout the place. "You have a daughter," he says quietly.

I nod. I don't say anything, won't tell him her name or any details. He lost the right to that information when he walked out of my life twenty-five-plus years ago.

"She's beautiful," he says, but I'm not feeling very generous.

I tap an invisible watch on my wrist. "I need to go to work soon," I remind him.

He looks down at his hands. They are strong and large but marked with the veins and spots of his age. They shake slightly as he looks up at me. "Will you sit?" he asks.

I shake my head. "I'm good right here." There's no way I need to be any closer to this man.

"I'll speak plainly, then," he says. "I'm not here to waste your time."

I lean against the wall and cross my arms, squeezing my eyes shut and thinking of my mom. What she'd think if she were here. What she would do. Mom was such a kind soul, but she had a sharp edge.

"I was a serial adulterer," he admits, pressing his lips together. "My wife Gail and I were high school sweethearts. She's a fantastic woman. Kind, smart." He looks at me and shrugs. "I have no excuse for what I've put that woman through."

I find it hard to feel any compassion for this Gail person, and I blurt it out. "How smart can she be if she never caught you in these, as you call them, serial affairs?"

He nods. "That's a fair question. Gail is a doctor. She ran a successful practice for many, many years. In fact, our nanny was my first…infidelity."

I open my mouth to respond but bite back my venom. I want to give him his ten minutes and then boot him out of my life forever.

"I ended up having three beautiful kids with Gail and three other children outside of my marriage. You were the first," he admits. "After your mother found out about my wife, she rightly cut me off from any contact with you. I won't try to make it sound like I was a good man, but I did try, Bridget."

I swallow the lump in my throat. "You had kids with three other women? Not your wife?"

He nods. "The difference is I was always honest with my girlfriends after your mom."

I'm stunned. Shocked, honestly. I drop down into an armchair across from the couch and shake my head at him. "What the hell does that mean? There are women who accepted being your…side piece?"

"Side piece…" he echoes, nodding. "Well, yeah.

They did. Gail and I were very successful, and I was able to provide for them. I was probably a better father and partner part time than a lot of men are full time."

"Oh my fucking God," I seethe. "Are you kidding me? You expect me to believe you're a good dad? A good partner?"

He shrugs. "I-I don't know what you're going to believe, Bridget. I'm doing a terrible job of explaining. What I'm here to do is apologize."

He pulls an envelope out of his pocket. "For years, I supported my children and girlfriends, and Gail had no idea there was anyone else. Until Ginger was killed." He tears up at that and takes a tissue from his pocket. He dabs his eyes. "Ginger was my youngest. I got the news from her mother about eighteen months ago. Car accident. Ginger was riding her bike on the way to school— she was a college senior. Middle of the day, and one moment of inattention and she was gone."

I feel bad for Ginger of course, bad for anyone who loses their life young and tragically. And I suppose this Ginger would be my half sister, but it's hard to process all the pieces of what James is telling me. It's a lot, and I'm starting to get nervous. It's nearly ten, and I don't think he's anywhere close to being done.

"When Ginger died, I told Gail everything. I fell apart. Starting drinking heavily, which is not good for me. I've had lifelong type 2 diabetes, was diagnosed back in my twenties. Anyway, I missed a lot of warning signs of things going on here." He motions to his torso. "Gail, as you can imagine, was devastated. Not only were there other children of mine out there, but to know that I'd been financially supporting two other families for all these years..." He sighs. "She left me, as she should have. But that's how I missed all the signs."

"Signs of what?" I rub my head, worry creasing my brow. I'm not worried for him, but for my job.

"Cancer," he says simply. "Pancreatic." He looks far off into the distance at a picture of my mom. "Bridget, I've spent the last eighteen months questioning everything I've ever done. I've spent nights drinking myself sick, crying, berating myself for everything I threw away. Once I finally got my sorry ass into a doctor and they told me there was nothing more that could be done, I decided the only thing I could do was try to make some of my wrongs right."

I shake my head. "So, that's what this is? You making your wrongs right? You realize it's way too little and you're decades too late. I'm sorry Ginger lost her life. I'm sorry you drank yourself into an early grave, but did you really expect to come here and tell me you're dying and have it make one bit of difference? How could you lie all those years? Why? Why wasn't the family you had not enough?"

"I know I can't explain it," he says. "I'm a selfish

man. Or, I was. I thought Gail having a demanding career and not as much time for my needs meant I should satisfy them elsewhere. It only started out as sex, but when your mother had you...I realized that I was addicted. To sex. To the chase. Maybe even to the thrill of being a father."

"You weren't a father," I spit out. "Not to me. And how available could you have possibly been to the kids you did raise? What were your kids doing when you were out whoring it up? How did you have enough time for three families!"

He nods. "I have no defense for my actions, Bridget. None at all. You're entitled to be angry."

"You're damned right I'm entitled to be angry." I rush from the chair and pace to the kitchen. "You need to leave," I tell him. "I'm not Ginger, and I'm not one of your kids. I don't care if you're my biological father. I want nothing more to do with you. Not now. Not ever."

James takes my outburst in stride. He stands up from the couch, the envelope he had in his pocket now in his hands. "This is for you," he says, holding it out to me.

"I don't want it." I shake my head and walk to the front door. "Get out of my house," I say. "Don't ever contact me again."

He stands in place, looking paler than he did before. "Bridget," he says weakly. "Please take this. Read it later, when you've calmed down..."

"Are you fucking kidding me? Calmed down?" I slam the front door closed, rattling the wood on its hinges. "I don't want to calm down. I don't need to calm down. I need you out of my fucking house!"

I feel slightly dizzy, I'm so worked up and angry. I storm across the living room and point in James's face.

"You, sir, whoever you are, are not my father. You're not a dad. You're a liar, a cheat, and, quite frankly, a thief. Do you know how hard Mom and I worked, how much she gave up to provide a stable life for me? Do you have any idea what it was like all those years without anyone to lean on?" I wave my hands around, motioning toward my house. "And you know what? The apple doesn't fall far from the stupid tree. I had a baby with a man who, likewise, couldn't give two shits about being a father or a partner or anything else to me."

Now that I'm talking, the words are flying out of me. I'm angry, sad, and I don't give a shit about the time or my job. I'm seeing red I'm so mad and sad. And if this man is really dying and he came here to apologize, I'm not going to let him go until I let him see firsthand what he's apologizing for.

"You!" I scream, pointing at him. My nose is running and tears are flying down my face, but still, I don't stop. "You deprived my mother of joy. You stole any hope I had of having a family and a stable upbringing. Because you didn't care about anything but getting your dick wet. I hate you. I hate what you did, the life that you lived. I'm sorry that so many people's lives had to be hurt because you were a selfish, cowardly piece of shit."

He does something then that completely surprises me. He bursts into tears. Body-racking sobs. His face is red, and his grief is so raw and so real, I'm taken aback.

"You're right," he says. "And Bridget, I am sorry." He sets the envelope in his shaking hands on my coffee table. "I'm sorry I disrupted your peace. Please read that when you have time. I don't have much time left, but every minute until I leave this earth, I'll be sorry for the pain I caused you."

He opens my front door and turns back to me. "Goodbye, sweet Birdie. I would really have liked to know you."

He closes the door behind him, tears still shaking his shoulders. And then, my father is gone.

17

CROW

ALL MORNING, I'VE BEEN WATCHING THE LOT FOR Birdie's car, but it's almost eleven, and she's still not in.

Tim's on the phone giving a client an estimate when Leo and Tiny walk through the door. Tim hangs up and runs around the counter to greet his brother.

"Yo, man." I nod at Tiny and give Leo a clap on the back. "Congrats, brother. How's fatherhood treating you?"

Leo is bleary-eyed but smiling. "Fucking amazing and insane," he grunts. "Morris is going to have his hands full in a few months."

"What?" Tim looks from Tiny to Leo. "Wait… Alice is expecting? Holy shit! Why am I the last to know?"

"Nobody knows yet," Leo says. "I mean, they haven't announced it yet. Morris was bawling like a baby when he came to see my son in the NICU." He chuckles at the memory. "He let it slip. And now, I let it slip. This is what sleep deprivation does. My brain is soup."

Leo updates us on Lia and their son, whom they have named Rider. They are both home and adjusting well, even though poor Lia is struggling with all the activity restrictions. While Tim talks to Leo, Tiny motions toward me with a nod.

"Let's check out the Crashpad," he says. "Lia's desperate to know things are going okay."

We leave the shop and walk up to the Crashpad. I'm shocked to see that Alice is inside, tapping away on a laptop while the dogs snooze and play.

Tiny yanks open the door. "Alice," he says with a grunt. "I'm checking up on things. Lia's missing the dogs."

Alice laughs. "Oh, I know. I've been sending her pics and texts all day. We're doing great. I told her to go sleep or bond with that baby. The pups will still be here when she's feeling up to coming in."

Tiny takes a picture of Alice waving at the camera and texts it to Lia.

"Well," he says, "my work here is done."

"Not a dog lover?" I ask, giving him a smirk.

"I've got three grandpuppies," he says with a sigh. "Let's just say I prefer grandbabies over grandpuppies."

Alice gasps in mock horror while Tiny heads back to the shop. I linger behind.

"Alice," I ask, leaning on the counter. "Where's Birdie?"

Her face falls. "Didn't she text you?" she asks. Then she looks concerned. "Something happened, Crow. She called me hysterically crying and asked if I could cover for her today. She said she was going to come in after she picks up Mia and Zoey from school, but I told her to take care of herself and check in later." Alice worries her lip with her teeth. "I thought you knew..."

Immediately, my chest caves in, and it's hard to breathe. What the fuck could have happened from the time I left Birdie until now?

"Thanks, Alice."

I'm trying to remember whether I said or did anything that might have upset Birdie as I grab my phone. I fire off a text and head back to the shop.

Babe, are you all right?

When I get back to the shop, Tiny, Leo, and Tim are still talking, laughing and sharing pics of Leo's kid.

"Tim," I say, lifting my chin to him. "You mind if I run? Be back in an hour, tops? I have something I need to take care of."

Tiny gives me a look. "Need backup?" he asks.

I shake my head, but something in my chest feels lighter. This is the brotherhood I expected. No questions asked. There for me, ready to ride into anything, no matter what. Somehow, with everything I've been through, with what I've done, the fact that Tiny doesn't ask means twice as much. That trust, that brotherhood, is stronger than ever. I'd like to think I've earned it, but it still feels like a gift. I clap Tiny on the shoulder. "Just need to head out and check on some shit. Thanks, man. I'll be back."

Leo nods. "Go for it. I'm sure my big brother is happy to not work and shoot the shit for as long as I can stick around."

I grab my keys and climb into the truck. I check my phone for a response from Bridget, but seeing none makes my anxiety level soar to new heights. I tear out of the lot and head for her place, my mind racing. I can't believe anything I said or did this morning would set her off. What I'm more worried about is that she's sick, in pain, or is battling a headache and doesn't want me to know.

The more I think about it, the more I start to freak out. What if she passed out or fell again? I shouldn't have left her alone after we had sex. I don't know how this shit works! If stress or activity or something else is a trigger, I got her into this mess, and I wasn't around to help clean it up. I drive as high above the speed limit as I'm willing to go without risking getting pulled over until I'm parked outside Birdie's house.

Her car is gone. I run to the front door, knocking on it with all my might and calling her name. I don't know why I'm knocking. If her car isn't here, she's probably not even home, but I'm at a loss for where the hell she could be. Did she drive herself to the doctor? Where would she take off to crying? I yank my phone from my pocket and start dialing her, but her beat-up sedan pulls to a stop in front of the house before the call can even connect.

"Birdie." I trot down the sidewalk to meet her at the car.

"Crow?" She throws herself into my arms and holds me close. "What are you doing here?"

"You never showed up to work," I explain, breathing in her scent. "I was scared to death. I thought maybe something happened."

She pulls back from my arms. "Something did, but not what you were probably thinking about. You can't run in every time you think I have a headache, baby."

I lift her chin and meet her eyes. "This is more than a headache. After this morning, I was...worried. Maybe you were..."

She lifts up on her toes and kisses me lightly. Her eyes are still rimmed with red and puffy from crying. "Regretting this morning?" She plants her face against my chest again and squeezes. "Do you have to get right back to work? Can you come in?"

I follow her inside, and the moment the door is closed, she presses me against it and kisses me hard.

"Crow," she whispers against my lips, "you don't ever have to question how I feel about you again. I'm in this. I trust you. I respect you. I want you. Do you understand?"

I hold her face between my hands and kiss her back, our lips tangling in a dance that's becoming familiar. And so, so precious. "Yeah," I grit out, "I do. And I feel the same."

"I'm yours," she says, a fresh shimmer of tears in her eyes. "And all of this that comes with it." She shakes her head and motions her hand toward the house, pictures of Mia, everything.

"I want it," I say. "I want it all."

She sighs, a deep sadness in her beautiful face. "Crow...I have something to show you," she says, taking me by the hand.

We sit together on the couch for a minute before she reaches for her purse. She pulls out an envelope.

"What's this?" I ask.

"This is my past," she says. "It's come back for me."

Fuck. I can't imagine what's happened, what she's been through, or what this envelope holds, but I'm here for it. I'm here for her.

Because she's a woman who can see past the paper-work, the record, into the truth, I have more than just freedom and maybe love—I have real hope. And I'm going to give that same thing back to her now and every day that she needs it.

"I don't need to see that," I say. "Whatever it is, I'm in. I take care of mine, Birdie," I say. "You never once flinched when you found out what I've done. What I've been through. You've never questioned my morality or soul, or even looked twice at me, even though you could have. Many other women would." I point to the envelope. "I don't care what that is. I'm here for *you*. I'm falling for *you*. I can dream about a future because of *you*. We'll get through it together."

A heartbreaking, fragile smile crosses her face as she speaks the words that gut me in the best way. "That's how I feel too. That's why I think it's important that you look at this."

She digs down into the envelope and pulls out a smaller item folded in half. "Start with this."

I take it and unfold it, immediately recognizing it for what it is. "A check?" My eyes are scanning the payee information, the amount, and then going back to the name of the man who wrote the check. "Birdie, what the hell does this mean?"

She laughs bitterly. "I know. I felt the same way at first. I literally drove all the way to the bank to deposit that and turned around. I don't know if I can do it. Read the rest."

I flip through the pages of legalese, and slowly, the picture comes together. It's a copy of a will. With it, there's a letter that's signed and notarized.

"This is from your father?" I ask.

She nods. The tears are gone now, but she looks thoughtful. Confused.

"He came by this morning. Right after you left."

"Fuck," I hiss. "I can't believe I missed him. I should have been here."

"It's okay. There's no way you could have known. He's dying. This is his attempt at making things right."

As best as I can see, James Sanderson has written Bridget a check for $75,000 as payment for back child support. For all the years he didn't provide for her while she was growing up.

"He's dying," I fill in. "And he's written you into his will."

She nods. "Along with his two other illegitimate children and the three kids he had with his wife."

"Wow." I hand the check back to her with my mind blown. "So, this explains how you're all related? Gives you the names and contact information for all five of your half-siblings?"

"Only four now," she corrects. She leans past me and points to the entry for Ginger Johnson. "Ginger passed away not too long ago. That's where she was laid to rest."

I rub my forehead, tiny spikes firing behind my eyes. "How the hell are you not on the floor with a massive headache?" I ask her. "My mind is spinning, and I don't know whether to be mad or happy. How do you feel?"

"Exactly the same." Her voice is sad. Conflicted. "On the one hand, he's dying, Crow. The man who gave my mother nothing but heartache, the man who abandoned me... He's going to be gone very soon. He's trying to make some things right. But I feel sick taking his money. It doesn't feel right to me. It feels like compounding the wrongs."

I nod and slide the check back into the envelope. "You should take all the time you need to decide what to do," I say. "Money comes and goes, but family..."

I swallow hard as I think about my own dad and how little effort I've made to reach out despite his many attempts. Maybe there's a lesson here for me as well. I've got the club, but that doesn't mean the flesh and blood Taylors don't exist. They are still out there. In their own effed-up way, I suppose they do care.

"Family is everything," she says. "Like what you have with the club. Morris and Alice—that's family. Mia is my family."

"And us," I insist. "I want that, Birdie. For us. And Mia. Everything I do is to make a better life for us.

Fixing your home. Teaching you how to make sweet tea that won't kill a man."

"At least I'll always find work in a prison kitchen," she teases.

I pull her close to me. "This money, babe, fuck it. You don't need it. You'll make it some other way. If you want to shred that check right now, burn that will, and move on with your life, just say the word and I'll find you a match."

She sighs and rests her head on my shoulder. "I don't want to burn it," she says. "I want to keep it. Does that make me a terrible person?"

"Hell no." I tuck her under my arm and cuddle her to my chest. "Why would accepting a gift make you a bad person?"

"It just feels weird. Like he's buying me out or something." She rubs her face and looks up at me. "But you know how this could change my life. I could worry a lot less about the doctors and medical costs. Take my time finding a job. I could even start a small business."

"Do you want that?" I ask. "Seems like everyone we know is their own boss."

She nods. "And with Mia… This money solves a lot of problems."

"It will buy some short-term happiness," I agree. "If anything, you can feel good that your father gave that to you. Maybe taking it will give you a chance to do some real reconnecting with him. If you burn it, it'd be hard to reach out and have a friendly chat."

"It's all so overwhelming," she says. She reaches a hand to my face and strokes my cheek. "The only thing I can say is that I'm so grateful I have you by my side for this. Whatever I decide, I want you there. Okay?"

I shove aside the papers and the check and pull Birdie close. I stroke the hair back from her face and whisper a promise against her ear. "Side by side," I agree. "We're in this together."

She lifts her lips to mine and we kiss, but this isn't one of frantic passion. The kiss is slow and tender. I nudge her lips apart with my tongue and taste her, and somehow everything feels different.

The way she tugs on my hair, bringing my face close, my hands spanning her back and holding her tight. There's excitement and electricity and all the same passion, but the thing that's gone now is any uncertainty. Birdie's mine, and I never expected that a man like me would get a second chance. Not with a woman like her.

Together, we'll leave the nest.

Together, we'll mend our broken wings and fly again.

And no ride has ever been sweeter.

EPILOGUE

CROW

Six months later...

I wake just as the sun is coming up. Birdie's bare leg is thrown over both of my thighs. I run my hands over the smooth skin, and she sighs. She rolls over and tucks her perfect ass against me, and I settle onto my side so I can hold her close. I curve my hand around her bare breast, and she giggles sleepily.

"It's so early."

I nuzzle my nose into her hair and breathe in every bit of my girl. My Birdie. The smells of sweat and sex from last night.

"I know," I tell her. "I'm going to go for a run. I'll be back."

I kiss her and climb out of bed, then dress quietly so I don't wake up Mia. I doubt she's going to get much sleep tonight at Zoey's, so I don't want to wake her up too soon. We have a long day ahead of us.

I grab my keys from the hook by the door and lock up the house. I spend most nights here now, but I still stay in my room back at the compound every so often. I think it's important for Mia and Birdie to still have mom-daughter time. When I'm around, we eat together, watch movies, and do our best to keep the noise to a minimum when we close the door to our bedroom for the night. But today's a big day for us, and I want to clear my head.

I bend down outside the front of the house and tighten the laces on my running shoes.

I jog a few blocks to warm up. I still use Morris's armband, and I've tucked my phone and some money into the holster around my bicep. After about a mile, I turn a corner and head into a coffee shop. An older man with dark hair sits peering at a paper through his glasses.

"You know you can read the news on your phone," I say, walking up to the empty seat beside him.

My father looks at me and just shakes his head. "I hate that device," he says. "I get my news the old-fashioned way."

I know he does.

"You want something?" I ask.

He shakes his head, but I know better. I walk over to

the counter and order him a plain black coffee and grab a bottle of water for myself, then join him at the table.

"Thank you, son," he says, eyeing the tattoos on my hands as he takes the coffee. Every time he sees them, I know it's like the first time. He notices them, wants to say something about them, but then stops himself. Today, he clamps his lips shut and takes the lid off the coffee to let it cool.

Then he goes back to his reading.

I uncap my water and sip it. The cold feels good on my throat, and my chest feels open, alive, despite the tension I still feel about my dad.

He's been in town for two months, staying at a short-term rental. He's planning on staying another month to help Birdie and me get her contracting business off the ground. She signed a lease to rent an office space in Morris's strip mall right next to Arrow's PI shop. She's going to be the owner of the business, and I'll be an officer in the company and her lead contractor. We'll have some hurdles to overcome with licensing and things, but we've got work lined up, insurance, and now an office, thanks to James Sanderson's start-up capital. That's what Birdie decided to do with the money her father left her.

Birdie's dad passed away only two weeks after writing her that big check. She did attend the funeral, and she met all of James's other kids. His wife. His other girlfriends. That was awkward and painful but somehow also very healing. Turns out Birdie's got one half brother who was working construction too. He's been consulting with us on everything from insurance to tools to bonds. And given all the siblings Birdie's met through her father, she might form a relationship with some of them. Oddly enough, James's widow Gail has been the one who's stepped up the most after he died.

I look over at my dad, who's blowing aggressively on his hot coffee, looking completely pissed off that the beverage isn't drinking temperature. That's my dad. Just because he's here doesn't mean he's changed. But since he is retired now, he's here for a while.

After I told him about Birdie and me trying to launch a business, he decided to come down and help us. Tiny put in some of his own start-up money to help, so it looks like the club will stand to gain from the business in more ways than just the rent we'll pay on the office space.

I'm literally going into business with my woman and my brothers. It's a cause for celebration.

"Party's today," I remind my dad. "You know where to go?"

He peers at me over the rim of his glasses. "I have the address."

I know Dad's not thrilled about coming to a party at the compound. He's got all kinds of preconceived notions about the club, what we do there, what kind of people we are. And that's okay.

Today, we're throwing a huge party to celebrate my homecoming, the new business that we hope is going to make the club some real bank in the coming years, and just all the good happening. Dad's been getting to know me again, and while it's not always comfortable, it's family. Both sides of my family coming together—my dad and my brothers—this feels like coming home.

"All right, then," I say. "I'll see you this afternoon."

I push the chair back, but my dad stops me.

"I've been looking for the right time to give this to you. I think now's as good as it's going to get." He is worrying me with the look on his face.

"What?" I ask, tipping my chin at him.

"You serious about this Bridget and her kid?"

I scowl at him. "Dad, would you just call her Birdie already?"

He nods and has the decency to look a little apologetic. "Sorry. All these nicknames just… I'll never get used to people calling you Crow."

"Fair enough. And yes, I love them both."

He digs into his pocket and pulls out an envelope folded into thirds. "I don't have a box for this," he explains. "Took it from the safe-deposit box and just meant to find something better than this for you, but... Maybe you can take care of that. If you decide to use it."

I grab the envelope from him and tear open the seal. Something small and hard nearly falls out. "Mom's engagement ring?" I ask. "Dad?"

He goes back to reading his paper. "Your brother's not going to use it," he says. "And even if he does get married someday, I feel like your mother would be happy if you had it. You know...for Birdie."

A sudden rush of emotion clogs my throat and I cough, but I quickly wash the feelings down with water.

"You know we haven't been together that long," I say. Not that I don't plan on making things official with her. But between her father dying, us starting a business with the club's and my dad's help, her inheriting both money and new relatives... There's not been a lot of talk about our future. A lot of happy nights and blissful days, but we're still sort of taking it day by day.

My father folds his paper and crosses an ankle over his knee. "Son," he says, looking me in the eye, "Why are you waiting to start your future? Haven't you lost enough time already?"

His words stun me, and not in a good way. I clench Mom's ring in my hands and nod, but Dad quickly reaches across the table and grabs my wrist.

"That didn't come out the way I meant it," he says, shaking his head. "I'm not... I'm not nuancing what I think. I'm sorry, Logan."

He releases my hand and scoots his chair back roughly. "When you went away, I thought...I felt..." He reaches a finger under his glasses to wipe at his eye. "I was sure what happened was my fault. Your tattoos, this biker business... It was all reaction to me. The kind of father I was. I blamed you for acting out, but I blamed myself more."

He looks me in the eye and shocks me by dropping a hand on top of mine. We're not holding hands, but he's squeezing the top of my hand, my sparrow covered by his, marked only by age spots and veins.

"Son," he says. "I've made mistakes. You've made mistakes. Life is too short to keep paying back debt. She's a very, very special woman. You deserve her. If you love this girl, take a chance on having it all."

I look down at Dad's hand covering mine, and I nod. "Thank you," I say. "That... It means a lot to hear you say that."

I get up from the chair and tuck the ring into the armband holster. I don't want to chance it coming out of my pocket while I'm running.

"Love you, Dad," I say.

He nods and unfolds his paper. "See you later."

I jog back home, where the house is already in full

swing. Birdie is taking her meds and eating one of the breakfasts she prepped last night.

"Feeling good?" I ask her as I kiss her on the cheek.

It took months of tests and trial and error, but it turns out the doctors are pretty sure that Birdie's headaches are the result of prediabetes. Since her dad developed type 2 diabetes around the same age she is now and there's no other cause that they could find, she's been trying to control her blood sugar and watch her diet to see if that helps ease the headaches.

"I feel great," she assures me, turning my face to kiss me on the lips. "But you stink." She swats my ass.

"Mama, that's so rude. You can't tell people they smell like that."

I ruffle Mia's hair. "Thanks for protecting me, kiddo, but I definitely stink." I down a glass of orange juice and get ready for the afternoon.

Once we're all dressed and ready, Birdie and I drop Mia at Lia and Leo's, where Zoey and Mia are going to hang out with baby Rider with Tim and Juliette while the rest of us party at the compound.

The girls have become even closer than sisters, and now that Alice is almost due to give Zoey a real sibling, we're planning on giving Mia bunk beds so she can have her best friend over any time Zoey needs a break from the newborn madness. Morris has begged for a bed so he can escape the newborn madness when he needs it, but that man is so excited to have a child, it's almost comical.

"Give me that smoosh." Birdie runs through Lia's front door, holding her arms out to baby Rider.

Lia hands him over and wipes her face with her hands. "Take him. Take him. Tim and Juliette are on their way, but I haven't even showered yet. Can you manage this maniac while I get ready?"

Birdie takes the squirming infant in her arms and loudly smooches his cheeks, making him crack up and drool all over her. "We've got this."

Birdie and Mia hang out on the floor, cooing and playing with Rider, who's doing his level best to crawl and jam everything into his mouth, while Lia's dogs bark up a storm in the backyard. Leo comes stumbling in about ten minutes later, his hair wild and a bag of diapers in his hand.

"You'd think we'd learn," he says, dropping the diapers on the couch. "Buy ahead, buy in bulk. What-ever we do, it's never enough. Is it just our kid who goes through like thirty diapers a day?"

Mia wrinkles her nose. "That's disgusting. Is it all poop?"

Leo kneels beside her and whispers, "You don't want to know, kiddo."

He runs upstairs to change just about the same time Alice and Morris knock on the door. I open it for them, and Zoey nearly knocks me over trying to get to Mia and Rider.

"And hello to you," I say, stepping out of the path of the flying child.

Alice, just days away from her due date, and Morris come inside. Morris picks up the baby so that Alice doesn't have to bend. They take turns smooching little Rider and making the kid laugh until Tim and Juliette show up to babysit.

"Is this the party, or is the party some place else?" Tim greets his buddies and even me warmly, while Juliette gives Zoey and Mia hugs hello.

Birdie and I leave Mia with instructions to behave and help Rider's uncle and aunt and to keep things clean, and then we all head over to the compound.

On the drive over, I take Birdie's hand. She's in the passenger seat of her beater, staring out the window as we pull away from Leo and Lia's.

"What's on your mind?" I ask.

She smiles. "Nothing specific. Things just happen so fast. A year ago, I was broke, alone, and mourning the loss of my mom." She traces her fingertips over the sparrow on the back of my hand. "I had no clue what happiness could be ahead."

I squeeze her hand and don't say anything. I feel the

same way, and while we have a lot ahead of us—work and her health—the future has never looked brighter. I have an idea suddenly and turn the car around and head back toward her house.

"Everything okay, babe?" she asks.

I nod. "Yeah, forgot something. Will just be a minute."

I pull the car up out front and park. "Come with me?" I go around to the passenger side and open the door for her. I take her hand and lead her to the front door, motioning for her to sit. The Florida sun is bright outside. Just like the day I was released, I can smell the faint scent of citrus on the air.

The heat on my neck feels so, so good, even if I'm starting to get hot. The fact that I can go wherever I want, whenever I want, is still a gift I don't take for granted. In the sun. In the shade. For a run. A coffee shop. The compound. My world has gone from a killer for a cellmate to a woman who shares her bed, her child, her home—her everything—with me. And I do the same for her.

"Here?" she asks. "Outside? Crow, what's going on?"

We sit side by side on the front stoop. The very same place where I first spotted Mia, crying and looking for help so many months ago.

I'm silent for a moment as I contemplate what to

say. What I'm feeling. I think back to that day. The man I was, running away from everything and into a future I couldn't have dreamed. Right here is where my second chance at life started. In a moment that was filled with fear and pain. Now, this stoop, this place, is home to me. A place of safety, happiness, and love.

"I love you, Birdie," I say. "You mean everything to me."

Her face flushes, and she leans against me. "Baby, I love you too."

We sit together for another few seconds before she looks me in the face. "Are you worried?" she asks. "About your dad meeting everybody from the club? We don't have to go, babe, if you're uncomfortable. I mean, I think it's going to be fine. Your dad can be a handful, but…"

As she's talking, I unlace our hands and pull my mom's ring out of my pocket and work it over her finger. "Dad gave me this this morning," I tell her. "It belonged to my mom." I meet her eyes. "I thought you should have it. Unless you want me to pick out something just for you."

Her mouth drops open, and she looks down at her hand. The ring is lovely, not a massive sparkler, but a modest oval set with tapered stones on either side. "Crow, what is this?"

"An engagement ring." I hold her hand in mine. "I was thinking we should—"

I don't even get the words out when she plants her mouth on mine. "Yes," she pants against my lips. "Yes, yes."

We kiss until I'm sure we're making a scene for the neighbors and my dick strains against my pants. We either need to go upstairs and celebrate privately, or we need to cut this short and head out to the party. Birdie has tears in her eyes as we walk hand in hand back to the car.

"I'm sorry my mother's not here to see this," she says, staring at the new gem on her finger. "She would have loved you."

"You think? I'm not exactly the type moms love." I chuckle, intending that as a joke, but Birdie shakes her head.

"No more," she says firmly. "No more poking fun at my man. No talking down about my man. You got it, buddy? I'm proud of you, Logan Taylor. You've got to start feeling that same pride in yourself."

I soak up her words as we pull into the compound lot. "One more thing," I say, needing to get this out and hoping not to get any pushback. "I want to adopt Mia."

"You what?" she asks, sounding shocked.

Once I park the car, I turn to face her. "Bryan's not a father. He hasn't been around or even called since I've been in the picture. He doesn't deserve something as precious as she is."

Birdie's eyes are filled with tears. "You'll have to ask Mia, and you'll need to get Bryan's approval—or however the court handles it."

"I have no doubt the asshole won't have a problem with it. It'll let him off the hook for child support."

"As if he ever paid it," she mumbles.

"If Mia says yes, that she'll have me as her dad, I want nothing more than to officially make us a family."

Birdie places her hand on my arm. "We already are, no matter what a piece of paper says."

I lean over, grabbing the back of her head and giving her a long, deep kiss. I almost get lost in her, forgetting where we are and what we're doing until she pulls away.

"We have to go in," she whispers, staring at me with soft, sweet eyes.

"Fuck," I groan, wishing we could be alone for the entire night, but knowing the guys are going to lose their shit when they hear the news.

"Come on," she says. "It'll be fun."

We link hands as we walk into the party, already in full swing.

Lia has a beer in hand and is clinking the neck of her bottle with Tiny. Madge is spooning food onto a plate for my dad, who somehow beat me here and is looking both uncomfortable and also totally intrigued. Leo, Dog, Eagle, and Morris all have drinks in hand, and when they see me come in, they roar in welcome.

I turn to Birdie, who has locked eyes with Alice and looks like she's bursting to share the news. "You good?"

"Never better." She kisses me lightly, then makes a beeline for her new best friend.

I'm standing in the middle of the compound kitchen, watching my father, my fiancée, and all my brothers together. It's the end of an era, for sure, when pregnant women, kids, and dogs become part of compound life. But somehow, it's even better this way.

I grab a beer and clap my dad on the back. "Birdie's wearing a little something you gave us," I tell him.

He nods at me. "I'm happy for you, son," he says and goes back to nibbling wings and potato salad from Madge's plate.

As I join my brothers, I feel for the first time in a long time what I've always wanted and never thought I'd feel. Freedom. Freedom to be happy. Freedom to forgive. Myself, and the people in my life who haven't made shit easy.

Freedom comes with responsibility and conse-quences. I know that much. But as I twist the cap off my beer and stand beside my brothers, I've never appreci-ated what I have and how I got here more. Birdie's smiling and watching me as she and Alice talk. She's got people in her life now—half-siblings and friends. Even Mia has changed in the time I've known her, now that she has a best friend and dogs and little Rider. Somehow, all of us together make a big, untouchable family.

It all started with a headache, a little girl, and a broken man who went stupidly into the unknown. Only this time, my instincts couldn't have led me into a better place. I may not have trusted my gut then, but stopping to help Mia and Birdie somehow made right my past wrongs.

I may believe that Birdie accepted me despite everything I've done, but earning my own trust back, believing in myself again, that's the real challenge. And it's something I'll work on every day for as long as it takes.

With her by my side, I'll be the man I want to be. The man I know I am. Flaws and all. I blow my woman a kiss and turn to my boys.

"Cheers," I say, holding my beer up so the sparrow on my hand looks like it's flying. My brothers raise their glasses and boisterously echo my toast.

"Fuck yeah!"

"Woo-hoo!"

That single cheer sets the fun loose, and the drinks start to flow. The conversation gets rowdy, and there's no better homecoming.

Celebration. Togetherness.

Good times and good fortune.

No matter where we came from or how we got here, we've got this.

We've got each other.

And that's everything.

WANT to know more about Crow, Morris, and the gang? Read **FLAME for FREE**, Men of Inked: Heatwave Book 1 and start your next favorite series.

Could you love a man surrounded by danger?

Gigi Gallo's childhood was filled with the roar of a motorcycle and the hum of a tattoo gun. Fresh out of college, she's about to start working at her family's tattoo studio — Inked. But when she showed up the first day, she never expected to run into someone tall, dark, and totally sexy from her not-so-innocent past.

Pike Moore is a bossy biker with a cocky attitude and an even bigger ego. He came to Inked to start over. New town. New job. New roots. None of that included coming face-to-face with the hot chick who spent a week in his bed before she vanished without a trace.

But when Pike's dark family history catches up with him, can he stop Gigi from being caught in the crossfire?

Download FLAME for FREE!

Don't Miss Out!

Join my newsletter for exclusive content, special freebies, and so much more. Click here to get on the list or visit **menofinked.com/news**

Do you want to have your very own **SIGNED paperbacks** on your bookshelf? Now you can get them! Tap here to check out Chelle Bliss Romance or visit **chelleblissromance.com** and stock up on paperbacks, Inked gear, and other book worm merchandise!

Join over 10,000 readers on Facebook in Chelle Bliss Books private reader group and talk books and all things reading. Tap here to come be part of the family or visit **facebook.com/groups/blisshangout**

Want to be the first to know about upcoming sales and new releases? Follow me on Bookbub or visit bookbub. com/authors/chelle-bliss

OPEN ROAD SERIES

Book 1 - Broken Sparrow (Morris)
Book 2 - Broken Dove (Leo)
Book 3 - Broken Wings (Crow)

The Open Road series is interconnected with the Men of Inked: Heatwave series. Learn more at menofinked. com/heatwave-series

Men of Inked
MYSTERY BOX

DELIVERED EVERY 4 MONTHS

SPECIAL EDITION PAPERBACKS &
EXCLUSIVE MERCHANDISE!

CHELLEBLISSROMANCE.COM

Visit chelleblissromance.com to learn more!

ABOUT THE AUTHOR

I'm a full-time writer, time-waster extraordinaire, social media addict, coffee fiend, and ex-history teacher. *To learn more about my books, please visit menofinked.com.*

Want to stay up-to-date on the newest Men of Inked release and more? Join my newsletter.

Join over 10,000 readers on Facebook in Chelle Bliss Books private reader group and talk books and all things reading. Come be part of the family!

See the Gallo Family Tree

Where to Follow Me:

facebook.com/authorchellebliss1

instagram.com/authorchellebliss

bookbub.com/authors/chelle-bliss

tiktok.com/@chelleblissauthor

goodreads.com/chellebliss

amazon.com/author/chellebliss

twitter.com/ChelleBliss1

pinterest.com/chellebliss10

Made in United States
North Haven, CT
04 October 2022